As he w̲o̲
arm glanced once behind him in time to
ing naked by the fire, her back to him. It was nearly dark
now, and the fire's glow bathed her backside in shiny
copper, her rump round and full. The side of one breast
peeked out from under her arm as she stooped to step
into her dress.

She glanced over her shoulder at him. He turned away
with a chuff. She giggled.

Meanwhile, on the other side of the creek, a tall man
with a rifle stepped out from around the bluff and hunkered down behind a boulder, poking his hat brim off his
forehead as he cast his gaze toward the camp.

Another, shorter man stepped up from behind him and
squatted beside him. He was beefy and thick-bearded, and
he wore an eye patch. He fingered the Henry repeater that
rested across his knee.

"Take him from here, Stony?" he asked, keeping his
voice low so that he could not be heard above the muttering of the creek.

"Not yet, Frank," said Stony Millen of the Gunn and
Cruz Bunch, the fire's glow reflecting in eyes set deep in
bony sockets. "Not . . . just . . . yet . . ."

TABOR EVANS

LONGARM

AND THE
BANKER'S DAUGHTER

JOVE BOOKS, NEW YORK

THE BERKLEY PUBLISHING GROUP
Published by the Penguin Group
Penguin Group (USA) Inc.
375 Hudson Street, New York, New York 10014, USA

Penguin Group (Canada), 90 Eglinton Avenue East, Suite 700, Toronto, Ontario M4P 2Y3, Canada
(a division of Pearson Penguin Canada Inc.) • Penguin Books Ltd., 80 Strand, London WC2R 0RL,
England • Penguin Group Ireland, 25 St. Stephen's Green, Dublin 2, Ireland (a division of Penguin
Books Ltd.) • Penguin Group (Australia), 250 Camberwell Road, Camberwell, Victoria 3124, Australia
(a division of Pearson Australia Group Pty. Ltd.) • Penguin Books India Pvt. Ltd., 11 Community
Centre, Panchsheel Park, New Delhi—110 017, India • Penguin Group (NZ), 67 Apollo Drive,
Rosedale, Auckland 0632, New Zealand (a division of Pearson New Zealand Ltd.) • Penguin Books
(South Africa) (Pty.) Ltd., 24 Sturdee Avenue, Rosebank, Johannesburg 2196, South Africa

Penguin Books Ltd., Registered Offices: 80 Strand, London WC2R 0RL, England

This is a work of fiction. Names, characters, places, and incidents either are the product of the author's
imagination or are used fictitiously, and any resemblance to actual persons, living or dead, business
establishments, events, or locales is entirely coincidental.

LONGARM AND THE BANKER'S DAUGHTER

A Jove Book / published by arrangement with the author

PUBLISHING HISTORY
Jove edition / December 2012

Copyright © 2012 by Penguin Group (USA) Inc.
Cover illustration by Milo Sinovcic.

ISBN: 978-0-515-15121-3

JOVE®
Jove Books are published by The Berkley Publishing Group,
a division of Penguin Group (USA) Inc.,
375 Hudson Street, New York, New York 10014.
JOVE® is a registered trademark of Penguin Group (USA) Inc.
The "J" design is a trademark of Penguin Group (USA) Inc.

PRINTED IN THE UNITED STATES OF AMERICA

10   9   8   7   6   5   4   3   2   1

Chapter 1

"Honestly, Marshal, I just don't know how I can repay you for all you've done for me," said Lacy Sackett, throwing her shoulders back and causing her red, scoop-necked blouse to draw taut against her breasts.

"All in a day's work, miss."

"No, really."

He was trying hard to keep his eyes off the girl's breasts, though he knew from previous glances and out-and-out ogling that they were fine and proud and firm, and that the low-cut blouse exposed a good share of the deep, lightly freckled cleavage. The nipples pushed determinedly against the fabric from behind what skimpy little under-thing she was wearing.

"Like I said, all in a day's work. It was my job to get you away from them owlhoots and that's what I did."

The tall, rangy, broad-shouldered deputy United States marshal known far and wide by friend and foe as Longarm swung down from the back of his smoky-gray gelding, squinting against the dust catching up to him and his beautiful blond companion.

"I just wish I could have thrown a loop around those brigands who kidnapped you while I had 'em so close," he added, staring back along the floury-white horse trail rising and falling over the sage-stippled hogbacks. He removed his snuff-brown, flat-brimmed, low-crowned Stetson and swiped it against his brown tweed trousers, causing dust to billow. "Oh, well. When I get you safely back to Jawbone, I'll head out after 'em again. I'll bring 'em in—don't you worry."

He looked at the woman still sitting in the saddle of her white-stockinged black horse, kept his eyes on hers, consciously not letting them drift to her tits, though he knew with his man's sense and his experience with women that she wanted nothing more than for him to appreciate her.

He winked at her, smiled reassuringly. "They'll hang for the folks they killed during the robbery, and for what they did to you, too, Miss Sackett."

"Oh, please," she said, her green eyes sparking in the western sunlight angling down from over the tall, rugged peaks of the San Juan Mountains jutting in the west, "we've been through too much together for you not to call me Lacy." She extended her left hand to him beseechingly. "Help me down, Marshal?"

Longarm gave an inward groan as she slung her right leg over her horse's rump and he reached up to wrap his hands around her slender waist. Her belly was taut and flat. As he held her, his hands slid up against the undersides of her breasts.

Yep, they were firm and proud, all right. He liked

their weight against his knuckles, however brief, and caught an imagined glimpse of himself cupping and suckling the naked orbs while he impaled her with his staff. When he'd set her down on the ground, she stumbled forward, and those two mini-volcanoes flattened against his chest. He could feel the soft, yielding rake of her nipples through his fawn vest and the blue wool shirt behind it.

She chuckled. Her chin came up and her green eyes met his. They were like twin jade blades of light that, while aimed at his face, bored into his prostate deliciously. Again, he heard an inward groan echoing around inside his skull as his pants drew taut across his crotch.

"Whoops!" she said, pressing her hands against his broad chest, her fingertips digging into the flat slabs of his pectoral muscles behind the flaps of his black frock coat. "Still a little unsteady on my feet."

"After what you been through," Longarm said, "I don't doubt it."

Reluctantly, he stepped around her and reached under her horse's belly to unbuckle the latigo. "Why don't you sit and rest while I unsaddle these horses? I'll forage for firewood and have a fire going in a bit. If I can find one, I'll shoot us a rabbit and try to throw us a stew together. It won't be no meal like what you're used to back in Jawbone, but I reckon we won't go to bed hungry."

"Oh, I'm feeling better now," she said. "Now that you've saved me from those horrible, horrible men." She stared at him, wringing her hands together, and gave an involuntary shudder. "God, how awful. Anyway, I'll gather some wood and get a fire going. I know how to do it. Daddy's taken me camping a few times when he went elk hunting in the mountains."

As she strode off through the brush lining the creek behind Longarm, he watched her over his shoulder as he unleathered her horse and then his own. Christ, what a filly! She wore that tight, low-cut red blouse and a very plain, long, wool skirt with rather plain, black, high-topped boots. But nothing could ever look plain on a girl with a build like that.

Lacy Sackett was the daughter of Alexander Sackett, the banker of Jawbone. The Sacketts were a rich family with a sandstone-block house sporting a wraparound porch and several turrets and balustrades on the town's ragged edges. Lacy had happened to be in the bank the day the Heck Gunn and Orlando Cruz Bunch had busted in, scared hell out of the bank's three tellers, pistol-whipped the president, Lacy's father, and emptied the vault of over thirty thousand dollars in gold coins and greenbacks.

Miss Sackett had been in the bank delivering to her portly father a wicker-basketed lunch consisting of a roast beef sandwich, a bowl of potato salad, and one pickled egg in waxed paper when the dastardly deed had gone down. They'd taken Miss Sackett as a hostage, threatening they'd kill the beautiful, well-endowed green-eyed honey blond if the town marshal followed with a posse.

As far as Longarm knew, no posse had been sent. And while the robbery and kidnapping was really none of Longarm's official business, him being a federal as opposed to local badge toter, and merely passing through Jawbone on his way back to Denver on the heels of another completed mission running owlhoots to ground, Longarm had gone after the bunch himself on the grullo he'd appropriated from a livery barn.

He'd also appropriated the black to ride in shifts with the grullo, allowing him to cover more ground more quickly than he could have with only one horse. When the robbery had occurred, he'd been enjoying a leisurely and long overdo bath as well as a three-for-a-nickel cigar and some Maryland rye, but when he'd heard the gunfire, he'd scrambled into action against the worried banker's wishes.

Someone had to do *something*, for chrissakes. Who knew what they'd do to his beautiful and virginal young daughter, though Longarm had had a pretty good idea . . .

He'd caught up to the gang after a hard four days' tracking and had sprung the girl from their camp early that morning, when she'd been stealing off through the brush to tend nature while Heck Gunn, Orlando Cruz, and the nearly half-dozen others were just beginning to stir from their hot rolls.

Now as the comely ex-hostage walked amongst the trees, stooping occasionally to pick up sticks and blow-down branches, he couldn't help admiring the stretch of long leg revealed by the skirt she said that Heck Gunn himself had cut with "an awfully large and savage-looking knife," thus making it easier for her to straddle a horse.

Long, slender, and creamy. No stockings to interrupt the view through that slit, either. Turning toward Longarm, she stopped along the creek and bent forward to

retrieve another branch, and her breasts pushed up entic-
ingly, damn near spilling out of the blouse. As they did,
she looked up to catch him ogling her. Longarm's ears
warmed and turned away quickly but not before seeing
the knowing smile quirking those rich, bee-stung lips
of hers.

"Marshal?" she asked a few minutes later as he
rubbed her horse down with the scrap of burlap he'd
found in his saddlebags.

"Yes, Miss Sackett? I mean, Lacy."

He turned toward her standing by the ring of stones
she'd arranged and in which the small, snapping flames
of a fledgling fire danced and smoked, crackling. She
had her arms crossed beneath her breasts, pushing
them up slightly so that a good half of those large,
creamy orbs were revealed once again.

"I just want you to know," she said sheepishly, her
cheeks coloring a little, "that no harm came to me."

He looked her over. She was unmarked. Maybe she
was too beautiful for even the lowly likes of Heck
Gunn, Orlando Cruz, and their motley, raggedy-heeled
ilk to bruise her up.   '

"I'm glad for that, Lacy. You got lucky. That bunch
is pure poison mean and rotten to the core. I've heard
about them from up Denver way."

"No," she said, shaking her head and lifting her
demure gaze to his, perfectly sculpted cheeks turning
the red of ripe apples. "I meant that they didn't harm
me . . . the way you'd think they might. My honor is
not . . . compromised."

"Oh."

"Yes." She smiled, then lowered her chin once

more, rubbing her hands together thoughtfully. "I . . . for some reason felt it important that you knew that."

Longarm found himself staring at her creamy cleavage again and gave himself a mental boot to the ass. "Well . . . I'm just as glad about that, though of course there wouldn't be no shame in it. There's not much a pretty young woman can do when set upon by the likes of Gunn and Cruz."

"No, I suppose not." Her eyes brightened and her red lips spread, showing the even white line of her teeth. "Do you think I'm pretty?"

He felt a thud in his loins, as though he had a second heart down there. He cleared his throat. "Of course I do. What man wouldn't?"

She continued to smile at him, smoke wisping around her, the burning sticks crackling . . .

"Well, then," he said, swallowing a hard knot in his throat and tossing away the sweat-soaked scrap of burlap. He looked around. The light was fading fast and a chill was descending from the pale-green, late-summer sky. "I was gonna see about shootin' a rabbit for supper, but I think I'll see if there's any fish in the creek yonder."

"I'll keep building up the fire."

"Sure, sure." Longarm walked over to where he'd piled his gear including his McClellan saddle and the more traditional western riding saddle he'd rigged to the black and crouched down. "There's some Arbuckles in my saddlebags here," he said, pulling out a fire-blackened coffeepot in which nestled a small canvas pouch of coffee beans. "When the fire's goin' good, go ahead and cook a pot. Me—I'm gonna do a little fishin'."

While the girl resumed gathering wood, Longarm produced a sewing kit he always carried for darning torn clothes as well as torn flesh. He plucked out the barbed fish hook he stowed inside with several sewing needles, as well as a length of catgut thread, then, tying a .44 caliber shell to the line above the hook, he wandered on over to the creek chuckling over the rocks at the base of a chalky bluff.

He fed a couple of worms to a couple of feisty, elusive trout before finally pulling one out of the little hole he'd found nestled against a gouge in the bank, under a low-hanging branch of a giant cottonwood. It wasn't a large fish, but it didn't have to be because the one he pulled out of the hole ten minutes later was nearly as long as his forearm.

"Oh, my gosh—look at that!" said Lacy as he dropped the fish in the brush. "You caught two lovely trout!"

He hadn't heard her walk up, but now as he saw her standing several feet behind him, he froze. The large fish flopped on the end of his line. But he'd already forgotten about the fish. The girl stood before him, barefoot and bare legged up to her knees, a blanket wrapped around her. Her honey-blond hair lay in a wonderful curly mess about her bare, porcelain-pale shoulders. She held two smoking tin cups in her hands, and she extended one to him, smiling shyly.

"Forgive my dress or lack thereof," she said, jerking her chin toward the camp in which orange flames danced in the stone ring. "I took a little bath in the creek and washed out my blouse. It was quite dirty. It's drying by the fire. I hope you don't mind my using your blanket."

She stared up at him as he stared at her, his hands suddenly weighing as much as good-sized boulders at his sides, making it impossible for him to lift them to take the proffered coffee. "Not at all."

She held the cup a little higher. "I brought you a cup. Thought you could use it. Getting a little chilly out here."

Finally, he regained some feeling in his right hand, and he managed to raise it and wrap it around the hot cup. She held his gaze, her eyes sparking coquettishly, cheeks dimpling. Then she said softly, sexily, her free hand tugging the blanket a little higher on her chest, "I'd best be getting back to the fire. Gonna get dressed." She gave him a feigned look of admonishment. "No peeking!"

With that, she turned and headed back to the fire with her coffee, the blanket sliding lower on her slender back. Longarm watched her go, sipping his coffee, then dropped to his knees to begin dressing the fish.

As he worked on the trout with his fold-up barlow, he glanced once behind him in time to see Lacy standing naked by the fire, her back to him. It was nearly dark now, and the fire's glow bathed her backside in shiny copper, her rump round and full. The side of one breast peeked out from under her arm as she stooped to step into her dress.

She glanced over her shoulder at him. He turned away with a chuff. She giggled.

Meanwhile, on the other side of the creek, a tall man with a rifle stepped out from around the bluff and hunkered down behind a boulder, poking his hat brim off his forehead as he cast his gaze toward the camp.

Another, shorter man stepped up from behind him and squatted beside him. He was beefy and thick-bearded, and he wore an eye patch. He fingered the Henry repeater that he rested across his knee.

"Take him from here, Stony?" he asked, keeping his voice low so that he could not be heard above the muttering of the creek.

"Not yet, Frank," said Stony Millen of the Gunn and Cruz Bunch, the fire's glow reflecting in his eyes set deep in bony sockets. "Not . . . just . . . yet . . ."

Chapter 2

Lacy insisted on doing the cooking while Longarm lazed back against his saddle with a cup of coffee liberally laced with Maryland rye, taking the rest she said he so richly deserved after springing her tender flesh from the trap of the Heck Gunn Bunch.

Of course, she hadn't called her flesh tender. That was Longarm's opinion, watching her crouch over the fire to fry the fish in his cast-iron skillet, shifting the fillets around with a fork.

He enjoyed the play of the fire's umber light in her honey-blond hair and how it shifted back and forth across her low-cut blouse, causing mysterious shadows to dip down into the crease between those magnificent orbs. He hadn't had a woman since he'd last left Denver chasing long-coulee riders in southern New Mexico, nigh on two months ago now! That might not have been a long time for some men, but for a man like Custis P. Long, for whom the soft flesh of a woman was almost as critical as food and water, that was damn near a lifetime.

He wished that Lacy would at least take the spare denim jacket he'd offered her, or wrap his blanket around her shoulders against the descending night chill. He needed some relief from the view. But she'd said the fire was all the warmth she needed. "For now," she'd added, glancing at him from beneath her honey-colored brows.

That had sent another spear of unadulterated passion through his loins, causing his longhandles to grow tighter across his crotch and under his balls. He squeezed his steaming cup tighter in his hands and took a badly needed sip of the bracing toddy. He thought he heard her chuckling but when he looked at her again, she was adding another chunk of pine to the fire, straight-faced.

There was plenty of fish, and Longarm ate heartily. When they were finished, once again Lacy insisted on doing the chores. She poured Longarm a fresh cup of coffee, splashed some whiskey in after it, and trotted off to the creek to wash their dishes.

Damn fine woman, Longarm thought. Damn fine. Almost wish . . .

Nah. He wasn't the marrying kind. Besides, once you marry a woman, everything changes. He'd heard about that stark reality more than a few times. Still . . .

When Lacy came back to the fire, she gave a shiver, then wrapped a blanket around her shoulders. She dragged her saddle over close to Longarm and lay back against it, and for the next forty-five minutes or so drank coffee spiced with the good rye whiskey and talked in a slow, leisurely way, sort of getting to know each other, enjoying the fire's warmth, pointing out shooting stars.

Finally, Lacy finished her coffee, set the cup down beside the fire to which she added several more branches, and proceeded to unbutton her blouse while staring down at Longarm. He stared up at her, one brow arched.

She didn't say anything until she'd tossed the blouse down on the ground near his crossed boots, had lifted the thin chemise up and over her head, and had tossed that down, as well. She had her back to the fire, so she was mostly in silhouette. But he could still see her naked, proudly upturned breasts rising and falling slowly as she breathed.

"Miss Lacy," Longarm said, tossing back the last of his own coffee and rye, "I do believe you're going to catch your death of cold."

She gave a shiver and crossed her arms beneath her breasts. "I would like to show my appreciation, Custis," she said smokily, "in about the only way I know how. Call me wanton, if you wish. Even call me a whore. But I wouldn't offer what I'm offering you to just any man. Only one who so bravely risked his life for mine."

She dropped to her knees beside him, leaned slowly forward, staring into his eyes, and lay her hands on his crotch, sliding them up and down his member that had begun hardening the moment she'd started unbuttoning her blouse. She flicked a finger across a fly button.

"May I?"

"Why not?"

Keeping her eyes on his, she unbuttoned his fly,

then poked a hand inside his pants. She shoved it through the fly of his longhandles and wrapped her hand around his ever-hardening member. Her eyes widened in surprise. "Oh, my! So . . ." She pumped it gently. ". . . Big!"

Longarm groaned.

She pulled it out of his pants and wrapped both hands around the base of it standing up now at full attention, firelight caressing the swollen head. He could feel his pulse pounding in it as she slid one of her hands very slowly up its length, gazing down at the fully engorged staff as though mesmerized. The night's cool air wrapped around it, relieved by the warmth of her hands. Her breasts sloped down against his right thigh, and then they mashed against it as she lowered her head, stuck out her tongue, which shone redly in the firelight, and touched it to the end of his cock.

He jerked at the thrill of her warm, wet tongue against his member and the pressure of her breasts against his thigh. Her hair shone radiantly in the fire's glow, as did her eyes, though most of her face was in mysterious, relentlessly alluring shadow. She rolled her green-silver eyes up to his coquettishly, still touching her tongue to the tip of his throbbing hard-on.

"Like that?"

Longarm grunted.

Her mouth stretched slightly as she smiled. "Bet you're gonna like this even more," she said in a taunting singsong.

He watched as well as felt her mouth close over the mushroom head of his cock and then slide slowly,

slowly down its iron-hard length. He threw his head back a little, grinding the heels of his hands into the ground on either side of him, the prickling of the pine needles and sand somehow enhancing the sweet, intoxicating caress of her hot lips sliding slowly down the length of him. When he felt the head of his shaft snugged tightly against her throat, he heard her gag very quietly from deep in her chest, her throat contracting sweetly against him, as she turned her head from side to side, as though enjoying the pressure of his cock snuggling fast against her tonsils.

Then she drew her mouth back and pulled her lips off the swollen head with a wet sucking sound. She laughed huskily as she drew several deep breaths, smiling up at him radiantly, then lowering her head again, thrusting his cock back against his belly and licking his balls.

"Ah, shit," Longarm said, gazing up at the stars, only vaguely noticing one arcing across the sky, shedding sparks, while her warm, wet tongue slathered his balls before sliding up his cock once more.

Again, her mouth closed over him. His cock slid deep, deep down into her throat once more, but then she pulled her mouth back to the head quickly and lowered it again just as quickly. Her head bobbed over his crotch as she slid her mouth quickly up and down his cock, her lips like warm, damp silk. Gently, she turned her head from side to side as she blew him, and he ground his hands harder and harder against the ground, his eyes open wide, teeth gritted.

This was how he wanted to die, he thought. Just like this . . .

When she had his blood boiling, she stood and quickly shed her skirt. Kicking it away, she placed a bare foot on either side of him and dropped to her knees, straddling him, leaning forward, lowering her head, and reaching between her thighs to wrap a hand around his cock that was so hard he thought the skin would split like an overcooked sausage.

He wrapped his hand around each of her breasts sloping toward his chest. The areolae were large, the pink nipples hard. The orbs were every bit as firm as he thought they were, pointing slightly up and sideways—a generous handful each.

Longarm sucked a sharp breath as she slid the head of his cock against her crotch. He could feel the silky tickle of her pubic hair, the petal-soft folds of her snatch as she teased him against her, making her wetter and wetter until with a little grunt she leaned forward and ground her pelvis down on top of his.

His cock slid up deep inside her. She expanded and contracted around him, like a grasping hand, and then she rose up and fell back down.

Rose and fell.

Rose and fell.

Her hair slid across his face and his chest, tickling.

If I were to die tonight, the lawman thought, *what a way to go!*

But it wasn't his time. He just wasn't ready yet, he told himself sternly as he closed his hand over the Colt that lay holstered at his side, under the coil of his shell belt.

Hearing the brush snapping around him, he slid the pistol from the holster just as Lacy ground her pelvis against him once more, squirming and grunting and squeezing her knees against his ribs. It took an extreme force of will to do what he did next, just as the girl lifted her beautiful rump in the air, sliding her honey-moist pussy to the end of his cock.

Raising his Colt in his right hand, he planted his left hand on the girl's shoulder and heaved her aside with a great grunt and chuff of expelled air while at the same time he drew aim at the pair of wolflike red eyes showing from the other side of the fire and just beyond its sphere of dancing umber light. The man-wolf crouched there shouted, "He sees us!" as he jerked a rifle up.

Longarm's Colt roared, and the wolf eyes disappeared with a shriek. As Lacy yelled, "Not yet, you sons o' bitches!" Longarm jerked up to a sitting position and fired at two shadows jostling in the trees to his left.

Pow! Pow!

One man yelped. Another cursed.

Longarm fired two more times at the thrashing figures, then heaved himself to a crouching position and, cocked Colt extended straight out before him, turned his head quickly from right to left and back again, pivoting on his hips, scouring the camp's perimeter for a full three hundred and sixty degrees.

Something moved in the direction in which the wolf eyes had shone. Longarm walked over to see a short, hatless man in a short bear coat crawling off into the brush.

"Hold it," Longarm said.

The figure stopped, flopped over on his butt. Blue steel winked in the starlight. Longarm's Colt roared.

The slug tore through the middle of the man's fore-head, basting the ground behind him with dark, white-speckled fluid. His head bobbed and then fell back along with the rest of him onto the ground.

Brush crackled to Longarm's left, in the direction of the creek. Boots thudded. A man wheezed and grunted, and then Longarm heard one of his bush-whackers wading into the stream.

Longarm glanced back toward the fire, saw Lacy stretched out on her back on his bedroll, propped on her arms. She was naked, sweat-slick skin glowing like brass in the firelight.

Longarm wagged his gun at her. "Stay put," he said, edging his voice with steel.

She merely shrugged as she watched him.

Reloading his Colt, he strode toward the creek, but by the time he got to the edge of the water, a tall man in a black hat was pushing up onto the far bank. He was limping and cursing under his breath. Longarm extended the Colt, emptied it quickly.

Bam! Bam! Bam-Bam! Bam-Bam!

The man fell on the other side of the creek with a thud.

Longarm turned back to the fire.

Lacy lay as before, propped on her arms, legs spread. He moved toward her. He stopped and crouched over one of the two dead men, touched two fingers to the man's neck. Dead. Stepping over the carcass of the owlhoot he recognized as Jim Riley, one of the Heck Gunn's bunch, he continued to the fire and looked down at Lacy. The honey-blond stared up at him, her eyes coy.

"How did you?" she asked.

"How long you think I've been at this?"

She shrugged her shoulders. Her nipples pointed at him. She had done nothing whatever to cover herself, and it rankled him. "A few years, I reckon."

"Hell, I spotted the mare's tail of dust on our back trail early this morning. When we stopped here, they pulled up behind the bluff on the other side of the creek. I heard every move they made. Knew you were only trying to keep me distracted so they could fill me with lead."

He squatted beside the fire and filled his cup with piping hot coffee.

"These three might be dead," Lacy said in a faintly jeering voice. "But there's plenty more where they came from, and in case you hadn't noticed, I'm a very valuable prize." She spread her knees a little farther apart, until a pink circle, like a small rose blossom, shone in the darkness of her snatch. "Since there's really no hope for you, we might as well finish what we started, don't you think, Custis?"

Chapter 3

"No point in goin' to sleep frustrated," Lacy added, wagging one knee and making that pink rose between her legs open its tender blossom still farther. She stuck the tip of her right thumb between her lips, and bit down on the nail.

Longarm stared at her. His heart began thudding again. Her long, slanted cat eyes glowed in the firelight. She wagged her knee. He looked around the camp. Except for the dead men, they were alone.

Obviously, Gunn and Cruz had sent only those three to retrieve their prize. Would they send more? If they did, they wouldn't likely show up till tomorrow. Maybe not ever, if the main gang decided to keep drifting without Lacy. After all, they had over thirty thousand in bank loot. That was enough to soothe the loss.

Longarm looked at Lacy again. His heart hammered

his breastbone. He kicked out of his boots and shucked out of his clothes. As he did, he kept his Colt in his right hand. Naked, he followed his jutting member over to the girl and knelt down between her spread legs. Just then she reached above her head and pulled a pistol out from under his saddle. He smashed his own pistol down hard on the Remington.

"Damn you!" she screamed.

"You think I didn't notice' that jake yonder didn't have a pistol on him?"

He tossed the Remington into the brush, set his Colt down just right of his naked right hip, and mounted her. She reached up and roughly raked her hands across the slabs of his hard chest, then ran them through his hair, snaking her legs around his waist and grinding her heels into his back.

"How did you know about me?" she said angrily, bucking up against him as he drove his shaft into her hard.

"That you were in with ole Heck from the start? I didn't know," he said. "At least, I wasn't sure until you started throwing yourself at me. If you'd been a little more ladylike, you might have kept the wool over my eyes."

He drove his cock into her again, slid it back, then pushed it inside her once more—slow, purposeful thrusts, feeling the heat in his loins building. She dug her heels into his ass harder, wrapped her arms around his neck, forced his face down to her tits, which he raked with his nose and bullhorn mustache as he fucked her.

"You bastard," she said, grunting and groaning, bucking up against him. "Oh, you fucking bastard!"

"Not very nice talk coming from the banker's daughter."

"You think I care? I was so goddamn tired of being tied to that house and that piano and my father's library, hardly able to venture out to the woodshed to stroke myself without Mother or one of the maids coming along to make sure I wasn't meeting a boy out there."

"How'd you throw in with Heck?"

"Saturdays my mother and that nasty ole father of mine—you should see the way he looks at me sometimes, when I'm wearing something as low cut as that red blouse you couldn't take your eyes off of!—hop in their buggy for a ride in the country, paying social calls on bank patrons. Good business, you know, to make the simple farm and ranch folk think they're Daddy's personal friends."

She chuckled and groaned as Longarm slid his cock in and out of her. "Oh, Jesus, you fuck good, you bastard! Your cock is twice the size of Heck's. Oh, shit, I hate you!"

She punched his shoulders as she writhed beneath him, sucking her lower lip.

"And . . . ?" he prodded.

"And Heck's bunch rode into our backyard one day. They were skirting town, on their way from a stagecoach robbery, and I found them winching up water from our well. Heck started sparking me, showed how much money his gang had taken from that Well's Fargo strongbox, and I told him I knew where he could get a whole lot more than that. And after he got it, my father wouldn't allow the Jawbone marshal to go after him . . . if he had me along . . . oh, *gawd, you're good with that thing!*"

"How were you so sure he wouldn't leave you high and dry?"

She smiled up at him devilishly as he thrust his engorged shaft into her harder and harder. "You know *exactly* why, you bastard!" She lifted her head and raked out an evil, echoing laugh.

After a few more minutes of their savage toil, she dropped her hands to the ground at her sides, lifted her chin, and arched her back. Longarm thrust against her and into her once more, rising up on his toes, and felt the sweet release of his seed jetting deep into her womb. At the same time, he closed a hand over her mouth to squelch her shriek.

When they'd finished spasming, he gave each one of her delicious breasts a brusque squeeze, then pulled his cock out of her and stood. Breathing hard, he tossed wood on the fire, then looked at her, lying there and hooking her hands around her ankles, rolling from side to side and staring up at him, moaning.

The fire brazed her beautifully.

Strange, he thought, for one so incredibly beautiful and beguilingly sexy to be as mean and nasty as a bobcat. He'd known bad women before. Plenty. But none that looked as pure and as purely ravishing as Miss Lacy Sackett.

"You won't tell Daddy, will you?" she said in a

frightened little girl's voice, half pouting, keeping her legs spread for him, fiercely coquettish.

Longarm felt the perspiration from their heated coupling dribble down his back as the fire caressed the backs of his legs with its warmth. As he stared at her—Christ, his eyes couldn't get enough of her!—he pondered what he was indeed going to tell her daddy. What was he going to do with her? A girl like her could do some serious damage. She damn well needed to be put away. He had to report her to the Jawbone marshal.

But could he do it?

She crawled over to him, climbed to her knees, her head about a foot away from his crotch and his long, thick, drooping member. She leaned forward and kissed its head. He jerked as desire sparked in him once more.

"If what we did earlier didn't convince you that you really don't want to tell Daddy about what I did, I bet, given a little more time this evening, Custis, I can make it very plain and simple for you." She blinked slowly and smiled up at him.

Longarm had to break himself out of the trance she'd put him in. Beginning to believe she was a witch, he stepped away from her and stooped to retrieve his balbriggans. "Enough of that," he said. "I'm taking you back to Jawbone first thing in the morning."

"You won't tell Daddy, will you?" she asked, still kneeling where he'd left her. "I mean, it's not like he'd believe you, anyway. No one in town would ever believe I'd be capable of such a thing."

Stepping into his pants, Longarm looked at her. He didn't doubt that what she was saying was true. Hell, he hardly believed it himself and she'd confessed the whole thing to him! Or maybe it was just that he didn't want to believe it because of the obvious hold she had on him.

And if she had that hold on him, a stranger, what kind of hold did she have on dear ole Daddy and the Jawbone town marshal and every other red-blooded male in Jawbone? Longarm buttoned his fly and decided he'd have to sleep on what he was or was not going to tell the menfolk of Jawbone about the lovely but troubling Lacy Sackett.

In the meantime, he said, "Get dressed and get to sleep. You stay put. If you try runnin' out on me, I'll bind you hand and foot." He went over and picked up the Remington he'd tossed in the brush. "And it'll be a long pull back to Jawbone draped belly down across a saddle. Got it?"

"Boy!" she said, cupping her breasts in her hands and looking indignant. "You sure are serious all of a sudden!"

Then she chuckled and started gathering her clothes.

Longarm tossed the Remington through the trees and heard it splash in the creek. When he'd wrapped his own cartridge belt and Colt around his waist, he retrieved the other guns from the two dead men lying at the perimeter of the firelight, then dragged both bodies upstream about fifty yards. The night predators could have them.

As he worked, he kept an eye on the camp. After

dressing, Lacy had rolled into Longarm's blankets and was now curled on her side near the built-up fire and appeared to be sleeping. He walked over and stared down at her. She looked like a damn angel, sleeping with her left cheek resting atop her hands that were in turn resting atop his saddle.

Her cheek was smooth and creamy, silky hair sprayed across it. Her shoulders rose and fell slowly, regularly beneath the blankets.

Asleep, all right. In his blankets. He was about to lie with her again, but he was afraid of the hold she had on him. And getting caught with his pants literally down if Heck Gunn and Orlando Cruz came for her, with more men. Longarm knew they had a good dozen in their group—all gun-savvy desperadoes who looted all across western New Mexico and southern Colorado and then disappeared for long stretches of time either in the Colorado mountains or Arizona. Possibly Mexico.

That's probably where they'd been headed when Longarm had caught up to them and snatched the girl away. The others were probably still heading south, Gunn having figured that the three he'd sent here were all that was needed to get his precious hostage back. Right now, the rest of the gang was probably well on their way to Mexico.

Longarm made another pot of coffee and sat on a log near the fire but stared into the darkness to save his night vision. He plucked a three-for-a-nickel cheroot from the pocket of his frock coat, fired it with a lucifer, and drank the coffee and smoked the cigar, pondering his situation.

He'd like to try to run down the Gunn and Cruz gang and retrieve the money they'd stolen from Alexander Sackett's bank in Jawbone. But the girl had thrown a wet blanket over that fire. He had to get her safely back to Jawbone. He had to get her locked up. If he didn't, he wouldn't be doing his job and he'd only be turning her loose to commit sins similar to those she'd already committed.

Or worse.

He wished he hadn't fucked her. That made things more complicated. Damn unprofessional, fucking your prisoner.

If only he'd been able to resist her. But she was no ordinary prisoner . . .

He turned his head to look at her sleeping there by the fire, her blond hair glowing as though from celestial light. He shook his head. What man could resist her?

He stared into the night and drank and smoked until his head was relatively clear. He decided that his first task was to get the lusty Lacy Sackett back to Jawbone, inform her father and the local law what she'd done and hope they believed him and not her. Then he'd send a telegraph message to Chief Marshal Billy Vail in Denver, recounting the trouble he'd incurred in Jawbone, and leave it up to his boss to tell him how to proceed from there.

That decided, he tossed the stub of his cheroot into the fire and, with his rifle on his arm, headed off to circle the camp a few times. Deeming the area free of predators—at least the human kind—he came back and shrugged into his heavy mackinaw. He looked down at the girl.

She'd rolled over in her sleep, and the blanket had fallen down her arm. He found himself lifting it back up to her chin automatically and chuckled. She looked as helpless as a newborn kitten, but in her heart of hearts lurked a dangerous wildcat.

"Thanks, Custis," she said, squirming around and clutching the blanket close about her neck. She smacked her lips, settled herself against the saddle and the ground, and soon she was breathing deeply, evenly once more.

"Don't mention it," Longarm said, giving a low growl.

He headed off to scour the trees for enough firewood to get him through the night. He couldn't sleep now, knowing that more desperadoes might be headed in Longarm's direction.

With the fire freshly stoked, he sat down against a tree at the edge of the firelight, rifle across his thighs, and sort of half dozed with his eyes open and his ears skinned. When the first light of dawn shone in the east, he rose, rebuilt the fire, then hunkered down against his tree again, waiting for the sun to rise. There was no point starting out until it was full light; he didn't want to risk injury to either of his two horses. Getting trapped afoot out here would make him easy pickings for Gunn and Cruz.

An hour later, when the sun was lifting above the eastern ridges, he rose, prodded Lacy awake with his boot toe, endured her cussing him a blue streak, then built up the fire. He ordered her to put some coffee on while he saddled the horses.

"Fuck you, you son of a bitch!" she fairly screamed at him.

"I made that mistake once," he said, hauling their gear over to where the horses stood in the trees. "Ain't gonna do it again."

She stepped into her black boots, grabbing the coffeepot and stomping off toward the creek. When she returned, he'd saddled his own horse and was working on her black.

"Longarm?" she said as she set the pot on the fire. Her tone had changed. It was almost polite, even demure. There'd been a sexy tinkle in it.

"Yes, Lacy?" he said with a wry snort.

"I've got a proposition for you."

Longarm glanced at her over his shoulder. "I already told you I wouldn't be doin' that again, but thanks for askin'."

"No—that's not what I meant," she said, standing by the fire and wringing her hands together shyly.

"I don't care what you mean," Longarm said. "Whatever it is, it's out of the question. You're headin' for the Jawbone town jail. We'll let a judge decide your fate."

He noticed that the black seemed to be standing a little light on one hoof. When he'd adjusted Lacy's left saddle stirrup, he pried up the horse's hoof to inspect it. There appeared to be a small rock lodged beneath the shoe. Just as he was about to pull out his pocket knife, he heard running foot thuds and lifted his head in time to see Lacy running toward him like an

enraged lioness, hair flying, face a mask of unadulterated fury.

She had a rock in her hand, and as she drew within
ten feet of him, she gave an enraged shriek and hurled
the rock with all her might at Longarm's head.

Chapter 4

"God*damn* your stubborn hide!" the girl screamed as Longarm ducked just in time for the rock to only graze his head while knocking his hat off, then thudding into the saddle stirrup behind him.

She continued at him, fists flying. Longarm straightened and let her pummel his chest while the black shied away with the grullo, both horses nickering and snorting their concern. The girl had landed one punch to his chin before he grabbed her, crouched, and threw her over his shoulder.

"Nope, goddamn *your* stubborn hide!"

As she kicked and screamed and pummeled his back with her fists, Longarm stomped off through the trees, heading toward the creek.

"Time for a bath, sis," he growled beneath her screaming and cursing. "Nice *cool* one. Start the day out right!"

"Put me down this instant, you big bast—!"

What had cut her off mid-curse had also caused him to stop walking. Gunfire. Several distant pops sounding little louder than snapping twigs. But then he saw a handful of riders galloping toward him from the east, tearing down a low hill, smoke puffing from the pistols they were firing into the air.

"Now what the hell . . . ?" Longarm said, holding the girl on his shoulder with one arm, his other hand wrapped around his Colt's grips as he stared toward the oncoming riders.

"Oh, my God!" Lacy shrieked. "It's Heck Gunn!" She punched Longarm again, harder, and kicked insistently. "Put me down—it's Hell-Bringin' Heck!"

Longarm set her brusquely down, then strode back to the horses tied in the trees. As the five riders pulled within sixty yards and continued closing fast, Longarm slid his Winchester from its saddle boot, racked a cartridge into the chamber, and stepped forward, holding the rifle on his shoulder and scowling toward the newcomers.

When they were within thirty yards, he dropped to a knee, raised the Winchester, and lined up its sights on the lead rider—a blond-headed man outlandishly attired for this neck of the woods in what appeared dark blue cavalry trousers and a fringed elk-skin jacket adorned with what appeared porcupine quills.

An ostentatious dragoon-style mustache curved down both sides of his mouth, and thick muttonchop whiskers framed his pale, freckled face. On his head was a tan cavalry kepi with one side pinned to the crown and a purple feather sticking up from the band on the other side.

Longarm blinked as though to clear his eyes as he kept his rifle's sights on the man's jostling figure.

The man's eyes widened when he saw Longarm, who'd been concealed by the shadow of the tree behind him, and he raised his left hand while with his right hand, which held both his pistol and his horse's reins, he stopped the long-legged palomino. A finer horse Longarm had never seen.

"Hold it right there, or I'll blow you all to glory!" Longarm barked, centering his Winchester's sights on the center of the over-dressed dandy's elkskin jacket.

The four other riders—all dressed more sensibly for trail riding but bristling with pistols, rifles, and knives—all drew rein behind the fancy Dan, obviously their leader. They kept their horses under tight rein, curveting the mounts and staring warily at Longarm, a couple looking ready to leap out of the saddles and dash for cover.

"Who the hell are you?" Longarm barked. For some reason—they seemed too slick and well attired—he didn't think they were part of Heck Gunn's bunch. "And what the hell you think you're doin', ridin' into my camp slingin' lead?"

Fancy Dan puffed up his chest and started to open his mouth but closed it again when Lacy came running out of the trees, exclaiming, "Dickie! Oh, Dickie— what are you *doing* here?"

Fancy Dan jerked his head toward the girl jogging toward him, and his pale face turned beet red with apparent relief. "Lacy!" He quickly shoved his pearl-gripped, silver-chased Peacemaker down into its greased holster and swung down from his hand-tooled saddle. He jogged toward the girl who kept exclaiming, "Dickie!" while Fancy Dan said, "Oh, good Lord—after what I'd heard in Jawbone I didn't think we were going to find you alive!"

"Oh, Dickie!" Lacy threw herself against Fancy Dan and buried her head in his chest, her face toward Longarm, and wrapped her arms around his neck. "Oh, Dickie, it was just *awful*!"

"Lacy!" Fancy Dan exclaimed, squeezing the girl in his arms and pressing his cheek to her head. "Oh, buttercup, I'm so glad you're alive!"

Longarm scowled incredulously at the pair, wondering if he'd been hit harder than he'd thought by the rock she'd thrown at him, and his addled brain was making all this up. The four other riders, still sitting their horses, stared down at the pair with expressions similar to that of the baffled lawman.

Fancy Dan jerked his indignant eyes to Longarm and said, "We saw this man carrying you like a sack of cracked corn toward the creek, and we thought . . . or I thought that . . ." He didn't seem to know what to think.

"Oh, that," Lacy said, glancing at Longarm then, as well. "Oh, he's . . . he's . . ." Longarm could see the wheels spinning behind her pretty green cat eyes as she formulated a story, more lies—and just what these would entail he'd be fascinated to learn. "He's the man who saved me, Dickie!"

She stepped back sort of formally, like she was at some highfalutin fandango at some senator's digs on Sherman Street in Denver, and swept an arm out in introduction at Longarm, who was still holding his rifle in his hands though aiming it somewhere around Fancy Dan's polished black boots trimmed with bright, shiny silver spurs.

"Dickie," Lacy said, beaming, "this is Deputy United States Marshal Custis Long, and yesterday morning at about this very same time, he rescued me from those savage brigands led by the cold-blooded, thieving killer, Hell-Bringin' Heck Gunn himself!"

Fancy Dan looked at Longarm, frowning, as did the other four men sitting their horses behind him. "Oh . . . yes . . . Marshal Beamer said a man who claimed to be a federal lawman went after you . . . against Beamer's wishes . . ."

"Yes," Lacy said, scowling. "Heck Gunn told Beamer as we left town—me riding across Gunn's saddle, which nearly killed me!—that if Beamer brought a posse, he'd be sending them back with my *head*!"

"So Beamer said," allowed Fancy Dan, still scrutinizing Longarm through slitted lids. "I don't understand, though. Why on earth was he carrying you so roughly over toward . . . ?"

"Oh, my horse threw me," said Lacy quickly, the nubs of her cheeks red as apples, which was probably how they always colored whenever she was lying, which was probably all the time. "And I must have had some kind of a spasm or some such, and the good marshal—Longarm, I call him since we're such good friends and all—carried me over to the creek, as he thought the cold water would bring me back around. But I reckon your gunfire was the cure!"

She tittered nervously, tapping a hand to her chest over her cleavage.

"You weren't harmed then, dear?" Fancy Dan said, placing his arms on her shoulders and crouching to stare down at her worriedly. "I mean . . . that awful Heck Gunn didn't—?"

"Oh, no! Rest assured, Dickie. Nothing like that. Oh, I'm sure he would have, given time. But I reckon the gang was so eager to get south as fast as they could that they were just too tired, the only night we camped together, to . . . to . . . well, you know—to do anything as awful as what you're thinking, but they didn't, Dickie. I assure you!"

Longarm heard himself grunt, felt his eyes roll in his head. Christ, what a piece of work this girl was. A true artist of lies and other sundry deceits.

"You're sure?" Dickie said, shaking her almost violently. "You're sure he—they—didn't . . . ?"

"Dickie, I would know, wouldn't I?"

Dickie stepped back away from her, dropping his lower jaw nearly to the bloodred neckerchief billowing down across the top third of his quill-adorned, elk-skin jacket. "Oh, God," he said, laughing. "I thought . . . I thought for sure they must have . . . Oh, *God!*" he fairly squealed, his right hand reaching for the pearl-gripped Colt so quickly that Longarm found himself raising his Winchester defensively once again.

But it was not at the federal lawman that the fancy Dan triggered off six shots in quick succession. Longarm watched in astonishment as the fancy Dan very neatly and efficiently blew six small branches off the end of a larger cottonwood branch about forty yards away from him, near where the creek flashed in the rising morning sun.

As the last shot echoed around the near ridges, Dickie twirled the fancily scrolled silver popper on his finger and stepped back, chuckling his relief and wagging his head. "Oh, I'm so relieved to hear that, buttercup. I mean," he added quickly, "I'm so glad they didn't soil you. Er . . . you know . . . that you weren't *soiled* . . . !"

"You mean badly injured?" she asked, smiling up at him cheerfully.

"Yes, of course that's what I mean!" Dickie grabbed his buttercup again and held her against him passionately. "I'm so glad they didn't injure you, dear, and that the wedding can happen as planned."

Longarm had a flash of memory of himself and Dickie's buttercup last night—Longarm driving her hard against the ground as he hammered away between her widely spread legs—and he heard himself groan his intensifying incredulity while at the same time wondering what it was, exactly, that this lovely little witch had up her sleeve *now*.

"Of course it can, dear," said Lacy, placing a hand on her chosen one's cheek. "I'm not injured at all . . . thanks to Longarm."

She turned to him, smiling wickedly.

"Oh, where are my manners," she said. "Custis Long, meet the man I've been promised to— Dickie . . . er . . . Richard Shafter. Captain Richard Shafter of the United States cavalry stationed at Fort Riley, on the Brazos River in Texas." She frowned up at the dandy curiously. "Or so last I heard . . . ?"

Longarm had risen and was now holding his rifle straight down by his side. As the ostentatiously attired captain strode toward him, officiously puffing out his chest, he said, "Yes, indeed, dear, I've been stationed at Fort Riley for the past year, but fortunately I was able to obtain a two-week furlough to come visit you. I was going to write but decided to make it a surprise. However, I was the one to be surprised when, only seconds after my stage pulled into Jawbone, I was told of the unfortunate turn of events at the bank and your kidnapping at the hands of the vile road agents led by Heck Gunn and Orlando Cruz."

He stopped in front of Longarm, squared his shoulders, clicked his heels together, ringing the jinglebobs on his spurs, and offered his long, pale hand. "Marshal Long, I will be forever in your debt for everything you've done for my fiancée, Miss Sackett."

Longarm shook the man's hand and glanced around the mustachioed dandy at his shrewdly beaming future bride. Or so the little bitch thought. If Lacy Sackett thought she was going to finagle her way out of being arrested, however, she had another think coming.

"Oh, I reckon it wasn't nothin' Marshal Beamer shouldn't have done," Longarm said, shaking the man's hand. The captain wore a gold ring inset with a green stone etched with two numeral eights. "The Double Eight Connected," Longarm said, releasing the man's hand. "That's a sizeable spread near Jawbone, ain't it? Run by a family of Shafters?"

"Oh, indeed, it is, Marshal," said Captain Shafter. "My father, Ezekial Shafter the Third, moved his herd up from eastern Texas just before I was born. I was raised out at the Double Eight Connected." He turned to smile at the smiling Lacy. "And I aim to raise my own family there, as well . . . once I'm out of the army and Lacy and I can be married, as we've intended since April of last year."

"You have, have you? Miss Lacy never told about no future weddin'."

"Why would I?" Lacy said, chuckling as she walked over and wrapped both her arms around one of Captain Shafter's. "I mean, we hardly know each other, Marshal. Now, since Dickie . . . I mean, Captain Shafter and several of his most capable men from the Double Eight Connected are here to see me safely back to Jawbone, you can go after Hell-Bringin' Heck Gunn and his gang, and retrieve the money they stole from my father's bank."

It was Longarm's turn to chuckle, which he did as he picked up his hat and set it on his head at the angle he preferred, tipped a little over his left eye. "Oh, you think so, do you, Lacy . . . er . . . Miss Sackett? Well, I got me another idea."

Chapter 5

"What idea is that, Marshal?" asked Captain Shafter. "I would think you'd want to run those owlhoots to ground. Why, if it weren't for my wanting to see Miss Lacy safely back to Jawbone, I'd go after them myselves. Bring them kicking and screaming back to Jawbone to hang from Beamer's gallows!"

Longarm almost chuckled at the dandy's ire, not to mention at the purple ostrich plume jouncing atop his hat.

"Yes, that's exactly what you should do," Lacy said, staring at Longarm, her green eyes and sharp and determined. "Marshal Long, you should go after those men and bring them to heel after what they did to me." She crossed her arms on her all-but-exposed breasts, then quickly glanced at her chosen one. "I mean, what they *nearly* did to me . . . and certainly would have done when they got to Mexico." Her cheeks colored a little as she held her gaze on Longarm, the only one in the group who knew she was lying. Brazenly lying. The only one who knew that she'd used her heavenly body on Heck Gunn in similar fashion to how she'd used it on Longarm.

To get what she wanted.

But why had she gone with a man like Heck Gunn when she could have been married to dear Dickie and likely inherited a Texas fortune?

Puzzling . . .

"Yeah, I'm sure they would have passed you around like a lone bottle amongst 'em, once they got to Mexico," Longarm said, shoving his Winchester into the grullo's saddle scabbard.

He turned a faintly cunning smile on her. "But I do believe I'll help see you safely back to Jawbone, Miss Lacy."

Despite that Shafter was watching him closely, a vaguely puzzled expression on his face that appeared to always look slightly puzzled, he let his eyes flick boldly across the girl's breasts to let her know he knew at least part of what she was up to, and that she wasn't going to get it.

"You and I have shared so much . . . er, I mean we've come so far away from the gang, I'm sure their trail's gone cold. Besides, ole Gunn's robbing the Jawbone bank is a local matter, not federal. Nah, I'll head on back to Jawbone, send a telegram to my superior in Denver, and see what his orders are. If I were to go after the Gunn and Cruz Bunch all legal-like, I might have to get sworn in by Town Marshal Beamer or the county sheriff."

Lacy tightened her arms across her breasts and glared at him, lips making a straight line across her mouth. Her pretty nostrils flared.

Longarm saw no reason in inviting possible conflict by informing Captain Shafter of his intention to incarcerate the man's wife-to-be until they got to Jawbone. If Lacy wasn't going to, why should he?

He looked at Shafter regarding him with that perpetually puzzled expression, red-blond brows furrowed over large, cobalt-blue eyes. "Why don't you and your men water your horses, Captain," the federal lawman suggested. "Then let's start the trek back to Jawbone."

Shafter nodded, then turned to the men still sitting their mounts behind him. "Court, we'd better water our horses. We'll start back to Jawbone in a minute."

When Shafter and the others had led their mounts over to the creek, Lacy turned to Longarm. "Well, I hope you're satisfied."

Longarm just stared at her with the faintly incredulous expression he'd realized was his customary expression whenever she was around.

"He'll kill me," she said, staring toward where Shafter and the men led their horses through the cottonwoods flashing gold. "Slower than Gunn, for sure, but he'll kill me just the same."

"How in the hell do you figure that?" Longarm said with a disbelieving chuff. "He looks as taken with you as every other man you show your tits to and wag your pretty little ass at."

Ignoring the question, she turned back to Longarm with a threatening look. "I could tell him of your intentions, you know. I could even tell him you took me by force last night. You saw how good with that pistol he is. His men are almost as fast and accurate as he is."

"Go ahead." Longarm gave a challenging grin. He knew she wouldn't tell the earnest, beplumed Dickie about last night. Hell, Shafter would more likely shoot her than Longarm.

She gave a groan of frustration and raked her hands through her hair angrily until that golden mass looked like freshly spun honey.

A half hour later, Longarm, Lacy, Captain Shafter, and the captain's four moodily silent trail partners were on the trail back toward Jawbone, a little town tucked between the Sawatch Range and South Park, along the Arkansas River.

The San Juan Mountains were directly behind them now to the south, and the Sángre de Cristo loomed high and mighty, like a long, giant backbone, to their right. The terrain they rode through was low rolling hills spotted with buckbrush and sage, with cottonwoods sheathing hidden creeks and piñons crawling up the slopes of buttes and shelving mesas.

The Sawatch towered ahead of them like gray-green, white-tipped clouds, ghostly in the bright sunshine and under a sky of liquid cobalt.

"Cigarette, Marshal?" Captain Shafter asked as he rode off Longarm's right stirrup. Lacy was on the other side of the captain, and the three of them rode point, the four cold-steel artists riding behind.

Longarm glanced at the small pack the man extended toward him in a gauntlet-gloved hand. On the package was a picture of a French soldier in a plumed metal helmet. The plumage looked similar to that of Shafter's own ostrich feather.

"Cigarette, eh?"

Shafter shook one partway out as their horses clomped leisurely along the trail. "Handy little things. Allen and Ginter's Sweet Caporals are the finest currently sold, to my mind. A mix of both Virginian and Turkish tobaccos. They're manufactured in New York City. A business associate of my father's sends them to me in exchange for stories of my skirmishes with the savage Comanche."

He chuckled as Longarm plucked one of the slender, immaculate-looking cylinders out of the pack. "A very fair trade, indeed—wouldn't you agree? I enjoy the taste, and I believe it lends an air of savoir faire."

Longarm sniffed the cigarette, which smelled a little like pumpkin pie to his sniffer, which was more accustomed to the cruder but cheaper three-for-a-nickel cheroots. "Wouldn't think a man would have much need for savoir faire down at a cavalry fort in Comanche country. Or anywhere in Texas, for that matter," Longarm added with a laugh.

The captain wasn't smiling, however, as he struck a match and leaned over with both hands, cupping the flame as he held it to Longarm's fancy-Dan coffin nail. "Well, damn," Longarm said, sucking a draught deep into his lungs and blowing it out as he studied the cigarette's neat little coal. "Different, but not bad." It sort of tasted like pumpkin pie, as well. One that someone had accidentally dumped pepper in. But it really wasn't a bad smoke if a man didn't mind looking like a damn fool while he smoked it.

"I hope you enjoy it, Marshal," Shafter said, bowing his head and cupping a flame to his own smoke.

"Hell, since you've given me one of these fancy coffin nails, an' all," the lawman said, "I reckon you might as well call me Longarm." He glanced across the fancy Dan at Lacy, riding with both hands atop her saddle horn, both eyes sternly on Longarm, her wonderful lips pursed disgustedly. "All my friends do."

She wore a striped blanket across her shoulders loosely, as the air was chill. Her breasts bounced strikingly as she rode.

"In that case, call me Richard."

"Will do."

Longarm glanced over his shoulder at the four men riding behind them—all dressed in denim and leather, and all with features carved from weathered granite, emotionless eyes set deep in hard, dark sockets beneath low hat brims. "What'll I call these fellas ridin' back here and lookin' so serious?"

They all scowled at him from beneath their hats, broad shoulders swaying easily with the gentle lurching of their long-legged ponies, pistols and knives glinting in the high-country sunshine.

"Forgive me," said Shafter. "Where are my mannners? From right to left, Goose Fallon, Orrin Brennan, Yance Studemyer, and H. G. Ryan. Gentlemen, say hello to Deputy U.S. Marshal Custis Long."

Even before the dandy had named the four men in his posse, Longarm had recognized two faces, possibly three, from wanted dodgers. As well armed as they were, and by the way their hands never strayed far from a sheathed weapon, he wasn't surprised they wore bounties instead of halos.

The hiring of gun hands on large, sprawling cattle ranches owned by men as land- and water-hungry as he knew Zeke Shafter to be was the way of the country. Wanted as all four of these cold-steel artists probably were, Longarm wouldn't lock horns with them on this trip. He had larger fish to fry here in the country south of Jawbone—namely, Lacy Sackett, who was probably more of a danger than all four of her husband-to-be's gun dogs put together.

A wolf in the fold, the girl was. If he left her to her own devices, who knew what other brand of cutthroat she'd throw in with without anyone in Jawbone being the wiser?

Captain Shafter took a long drag off his Sweet Caporal, blew the smoke out his fine patrician's nose, and said, "As soon as I pulled into Jawbone and heard that Heck Gunn and that jasper, Orlando Cruz, had taken Lacy, I sent for my father's four top hands straight away! Not but the finest for my buttercup."

The dandified Captain gave Lacy a wink, which set her to beaming.

"Howdy, fellas," Longarm said with a disarming smile, pinching his hat brim to Fallon, Brennan, Studemyer, and Ryan. "Since we're all gonna be trailin' together a few days, you might as well call me Longarm."

The dull looks they gave him caused him to make a mental note to sleep lightly and keep a close eye on his back.

*   *   *

They rode until an hour before dark and made camp
along a creek that ran out from the Sangre de Cristo
to carve a meandering path across the San Juan valley.
No one said much of anything—at least no one
amongst Longarm and Shafter's four cold-steel artists,
though they infrequently spoke amongst themselves
tonelessly, half-grunting, half-speaking in clipped
phrases, eyeing Longarm darkly.

Lacy and her Dickie, however, spoke plenty though
only to each other. Long before they'd made camp, Longarm had grown nearly physically ill at their carrying-on
like a couple of schoolchildren—the whispers, snickers,
quick kisses, Shafter's intimate chuckles and Lacy's
responsive giggles or playfully chiding swipes across
his shoulder.

The way she was acting, as though she still
intended to marry Richard Shafter, made Longarm
wonder why she didn't. Or at least *hadn't* intended to
marry him and had thrown in with Heck Gunn and
Orlando Cruz.

She'd said Shafter was going to kill her, but from
what Longarm could see, the man was about as starry-
eyed about her as a man could be about a girl. For
chrissakes, the dandy was making a fool of himself in
front of Longarm and his four stony-eyed pistoleros!
He couldn't help himself, it seemed.

Maybe Lacy Sackett was not only diabolical but
crazy, as well.

After they'd all had a supper of roasted rabbit and
coffee, Longarm checked on his horse once more
where it was tended with the others, then took a wide

swing around the encampment to make sure there were no interlopers skulking about. He wasn't entirely convinced that Heck Gunn and his kill-crazy *compañero*, Cruz, had continued on south when their three bushwhackers hadn't returned with Lacy.

Men like Gunn and Cruz didn't cotton to losing battles. And most certainly not women. Especially not ones who filled a blouse the way Lacy Sackett did.

Finding nothing more threatening than a couple of coyotes hunting a wash that branched off from the main creek, Longarm headed back to the campfire. As he did, he spied Shafter and Lacy walking arm in arm along the creek, the last dying rays of the day glistening in the girl's hair as well as in the ostrich feather bobbing and weaving atop the captain's tan kepi.

She had her striped blanket wrapped around her bare shoulders. In the heavy night silence, he could hear them muttering little annoying intimacies into each other's ears and snickering like a nine-year-olds with foot fetishes playing doctor in the wood shed.

Longarm walked on back to the camp where the four gunslicks were lounging against their saddles on one side of the fire, playing poker and muttering amongst themselves though in decidedly less intimate tones than those of Lacy and the captain. No one invited Longarm to join the game, so he had another cup of coffee laced with rye, sitting by himself a ways from the camp, then rolled up in his blankets.

He slept with one ear skinned and one eye almost virtually open but had still managed to drift into a restful slumber when he was awakened suddenly by Lacy's shrill, echoing screech.

Chapter 6

Longarm bolted to his feet, Colt in hand.

Heart thudding, crouching, feet spread, ready for action, he looked around. Shafter's four gunmen were all in similar poses, one or two pistols extended by each. The fire had burned down to umber coals, casting them all in silhouette.

The night beyond the fire was inky black though as Longarm's eyes slowly adjusted, he could make out a few details—trees, branches, leaves, pale rocks, the silvery-blue line of the creek about thirty yards beyond the camp. The shallow, slow-moving stream made a gentle murmur. Otherwise there were no sounds except the breathing of the four gunmen and the faint crackling of the fire's coals.

The girl whimpered from somewhere off ahead of Longarm and to his right, southwest of the camp. He started running, boots thudding softly. The others came after him, no one saying anything, the air around them tense and expectant. Starlight glistened weakly off their extended pistols.

Longarm stopped, turning an ear in the direction the girl's scream had come from.

Longarm was beginning to think he'd imagined the screech and ensuing whimper when there was another sound—deeper this time and obviously caused by Lacy drawing a ragged breath.

Longarm continued forward and stopped near a broad juniper. Just as he held a branch aside and peered through the tree, a man grunted, sighed, and then Longarm knew what had caused the commotion.

About twenty feet beyond him, a low fire burned. Two silhouettes hunkered down between Longarm and the fire—one that Longarm recognized as Lacy kneeling bent forward, her ass in the air. Her hair shone in the firelight.

The other pale shadow belonged to Shafter, who, wearing only his hat, knelt behind her. The captain had his hands on the girl's hips, and grinding his pelvis against her ass, he grunted softly and jerked while she continued to whimper with satisfaction.

Longarm released the branch with a disgusted chuff and turned toward the men spread out behind him. "False alarm, amigos."

He depressed the Colt's hammer, shoved it down into its holster, and started walking back to the fire. The gunmen lingered behind him, peering through the juniper, snorting and chuckling.

The tall, lanky pistoleer called Goose said, "Suppose he's gonna give us each a turn?"

Another man snorted.

"Hell, that weren't no love scream," the man called Ryan said as they walked slowly back to their own fire behind Longarm. "Now, me—I could make that pretty little puss really *meow!*"

More snorts and muffled laughter.

While the others settled back down in their own soogans on the other side of the fire ring, muttering amongst themselves, Longarm slacked down into his own bedroll. He leaned back against his saddle and crossed his arms on his chest. He stared at the stars through the thin vapor of his own breath.

Something was eating at him. What was it?

Lacy.

He chewed his mustache as he recognized the emotion despite his having felt it but maybe once or twice in his life before.

Jealousy.

Lacy gave another groan as the captain finished. On the quiet night air, he could hear them speaking in hushed tones. He said something and she gave a husky laugh. Suddenly their fire flared as one of them added more wood to it.

He couldn't help remembering his own night with the diabolical vixen. Even knowing how evil she was—or maybe because of it—he'd had one hell of a fine, old time between her legs, enjoying her warm, soft lips and teasing tongue on his pecker. Now she was giving all that to Captain Shafter, and while Longarm felt no emotional pull toward the girl, he did feel an ache in his crotch, and that was enough to cause him to bite down hard on his back teeth and give a deep, ragged sigh as he tipped his hat down low over his eyes and beckoned sleep.

The four gunmen must have been suffering a similar frustration. He could hear them about twenty feet beyond him, whispering and chuckling, expressing their own goatish desires. Longarm grinned at the next thought that entered his head.

The captain better watch himself with that demonic little filly, he thought, or he's liable to end up with a bullet in his head.

"Sleep well, Longarm?" she asked the next day just after sunrise, when he and the four gunmen were rigging their horses.

She strolled up to him wearing one of the captain's spare shirts—a brown wool shirt trimmed with red piping that she'd left about half unbuttoned and knotted around her waist, leaving about two inches of her midriff bare. The shirt was pulled taught against the two round mounds of her jutting breasts.

Her freshly brushed hair glistened like honey with buttery sunlight shining through it.

Longarm ignored the twinge of desire in the head of his otherwise slack cock.

"There's nothing like the cool night air for helping a man to a good night's rest," he said, puffing a three-for-a-nickel cheroot as he tied his bedroll behind his saddle.

She stopped a few feet away from him, crossing her arms beneath her breasts and cocking one leg forward, glancing back to where the captain sat on a rock,

enjoying a cup of coffee and one of his prissy ciga-
rettes. "Dickie slept well, also. After he finally got to
sleep, I mean. I don't think the percentage gals down
Texas way can satisfy him—not after enjoying the
pleasure of *moi* in Jawbone. So we had a reunion of
sorts. I hope I didn't scream too loudly."

"Oh, did you scream?"

"Fuck you," she said softly through a crooked smile.
"You know I did. But I was thinking about you, Longarm. And that plow handle you battered me with the
night before."

Longarm didn't look at her, hoping she'd go away, as
he tied the second strap on his hot roll. The other men
were several yards away, smoking and tending their own
mounts, one cleaning out the frog of his skewbald
paint's left front hoof.

She stepped up beside Longarm and whispered just
off his left shoulder, "You could have me again, if you
wanted me badly enough. Me . . . and so much more,
Custis." She pivoted coquettishly, giving him a saucy
look as she swung her hair back, then started back
toward Shafter, saying quietly over her shoulder to
Longarm, "I reckon you're just going to have to want
it again badly enough, aren't you?"

Longarm almost choked on the raw knot in his throat
as he pulled the strap taut on his bedroll. His knees felt
like sponges, and a vein in his temple throbbed. He
could hear her behind him, talking in sultry tones with
Shafter, and he hated the way he hated it. Hated her and
hated Shafter.

The girl needed to be locked up, the key thrown in
the ocean.

He backed his grullo out away from the other horses and stepped into the saddle. He glanced down at where the captain sat on a rock near the fire they'd built up for breakfast and had Lacy on his knee. They both looked up at him.

"I'm gonna ride back a few miles, make sure we haven't been followed by Gunn and Cruz's bunch."

"Well, I for one applaud your decision, Marshal!" said the fancy Dan, widening his eyes and puffing out his too-thin chest behind that silly elk-skin jacket that made him look like a younger, sillier version of Buffalo Bill Cody.

Lacy wrapped her arms around his neck and beamed at him. She slid her eyes once, snidely, toward Longarm, then slid them back to Shafter as if the gaudy, overwrought sissy were the man of her dreams.

Longarm pinched his hat brim to the pair, then reined the grullo away from the fire and loped it back out to the main trail, the four gunmen looking after him curiously. When he was half a mile out from the camp, he started feeling better, looser. Or at least not as tight.

Christ, that girl had a hold on him. But what man wouldn't she have a hold on? He'd known a few women like that—women you could fall in love with after a single glance, as though that glance were a net they dropped over you, tightened up like Glidden wire and with which they drew you toward them and held you there, under an otherwordly spell you couldn't break free of.

Of course, it was a net that in reality men really only threw over themselves and paid dearly for doing

it. But it couldn't be helped. Girls like Lacy Sackett—
and there were damn few of her caliber—quickly
became the objects of men's obsessions. Often several
men at once. And they knew it from an early age, and
they took full advantage of it.

Why the hell not?

As he put the horse up a long, low rise straight south
of where he and the others had bivouacked, he came
to the rock-hard conclusion that this girl, Lacy Sackett,
was more of a succubus than any other siren on earth
or elsewhere. This one really was a witch. Pure-dee
dyed-in-the-wool evil.

He snorted a wry, mirthless laugh.

And what he wouldn't give to be able to let his
guard down and have her writhing under him one more
time!

He rode for another mile. To his right lay a shelving
mesa about the size of a small frontier settlement. It
resembled a sinking ship, and he rode up the sunken
end to the prow of steep, crenelated sandstone.

Dismounting the grullo, he reached into his saddlebags and pulled out a pair of army field glasses. He
hunkered down behind a boulder at the lip of the mesa
and cast his gaze out over the top of the rock to the
south, adjusting the glasses' focus until he had clear,
broad view of his and the others' back trail for a couple of miles.

He studied the broad valley closely, spying nothing but two riders heading from his left to his right
about a mile away. They were trailing a small herd of
horses and likely worked for one of the area's sprawling ranches. The only other movement was a trio of

coyotes and several rabbits scuttling about between sage clumps.

He'd just started to lower the glasses when something moved. He steadied them, turning slightly left until he brought up several riders riding toward him along his and the others' back trail. His heart quickened. He continued to steady the glasses and squint through the two semicircles of magnified terrain. The figures themselves were loping their mounts, rising up and down, but as they came down a rise Longarm could make out the two lead riders.

Heck Gunn was on the left, wearing his customary opera hat with a spray of wildflowers rising from the silk band around the crown. He also wore round-rimmed, steel-framed glasses, and a gold hoop ring dangled from his right ear.

Orlando Cruz rode to Gunn's left—a stocky Mexican in a bowler hat, with long black hair hanging to his shoulders, and cartridge bandoliers crisscrossed on his chest, over a short, Mexican-style leather jacket. He rode with a sawed-off shotgun hanging down his chest by a leather lanyard. Gunn's own arsenal included three pistols holstered on his hips and over his belly.

The ten or so men behind him and Gunn were similarly attired and armed. A rugged, mean, nasty bunch. And they were after Lacy. Sure enough, they had to be. What else could lure them back north—back in the direction of the last bank they'd robbed—instead of south to the safety and anonymity of Mexico?

Gunn and Cruz and maybe all the others had gotten a taste of something they needed more of.

Longarm lowered the glasses, rose, and dropped

them back into his saddlebags. He swung into the saddle and gigged the grullo back down the slanting mesa to the tableland, then turned the horse right, heading back to the trail.

As he did, he glanced behind him. He couldn't see the men trailing him from nearly a mile away, but they were pushing their horses hard. If they kept up that frantic pace, they'd be on Shafter's group soon. Longarm had to reach them and warn them. With Shafter's four gunnies, Shafter himself, and Longarm, they should be able to bring down Heck Gunn and Orlando Cruz handily, and then Longarm would not only have captured their deceitful albeit beautiful coconspirator, but he'd have the money they'd stolen from Alexander Sackett's bank, as well.

He tapped the heels of his cavalry stovepipes against the grullo's flanks, and the horse responded by stretching its stride into a sage-chewing gallop straight north along the old Indian trail he and the others had followed. He was starting to feel better, less like a damn sap and more like a lawman again, when he, staring straight ahead over his lunging horse's head and twitching ears, saw something that created an instant ache in the pit of his belly.

Someone lying beside the trail near where he and the others had camped the night before.

He knew right away who it was. Some inner voice told him, and when he'd swung down from the grullo while it was still running, he dropped to a knee beside the man and saw the fringed elk-skin jacket, the red-blond hair curling over the collar.

Shafter lay on his side. He was still breathing, his

shoulders rising and falling quickly. With every breath, he shuddered.

Longarm rolled him over on his back and winced when he saw the blood over the man's belly. The fancy Dan had both his gloved hands clamped tight to the wound, but they weren't stopping the blood and viscera from oozing out of the two or three holes in him. His open eyes were vacant, but they swung toward Longarm, and his mouth opened and closed as he managed to say, "B-bastards . . . took her. Took . . . Lacy."

"Why?" But of course Longarm knew why. They wanted some of what they'd heard last night for themselves.

"They laughed," Shafter said. "They just kept . . . laughing . . ."

"Do you know where they're headed?"

All Captain Richard Shafter said was, "B-bastards . . ." And then he turned his head to one side, and his shoulders stopped rising and falling. His hands fell away from his belly.

Longarm cursed and looked down his back trail. The pack of Gunn and Cruz riders were merely a brown splotch from this distance. It was hard to tell, but Longarm thought they were walking their horses.

He turned back to Shafter, shook his head in frustration. "You stupid son of a bitch, Dickie!" If the man hadn't been lording the girl over his men, this might not have happened. Now, Longarm had a decision to make. Did he want to try to ambush Gunn and Cruz and retrieve the stolen money or go after Lacy?

He didn't have much sympathy for the girl, but it was her he'd go after. He couldn't let Dickie's four gunnies rape her and likely kill her and toss her in some ravine. Gunn and Cruz's men could wait. At least, he'd save them for later if they didn't catch up to him before he'd caught up to Lacy and her four captors . . .

Quickly, he dragged the dead Dickie Shafter off the trail and behind a knoll. "Sorry, pal. I'd like to dig you a proper grave, but we're burnin' daylight."

Longarm merely laid the man out as respectfully as he could—on his back, legs together, wrists crossed on his bloody belly—then jogged back out to where his grullo cropped fescue and buckbrush. Swinging into the saddle, he glanced behind once more.

Gunn and Cruz were no longer visible, having most likely dropped into a crease between low prairie swells. They were back there, though. They had to be. And since Longarm didn't have time to cover his and the four gunmen's tracks, they'd be tracking him as he tracked them until they eventually caught up to him.

And then, if his current streak of sour luck continued, he'd likely be caught in one hell of a cross fire.

Chapter 7

The night was cold as a grave digger's ass.

Cold moonlight reflected off the sheer peaks rising around Longarm, jutting tall above the pines and firs crowding close to the trail, the stony crests hidden far above. A lone wolf howled—a mournful, bewitching sound on such a cold, moonlit night this far up in the high and rocky.

The pine boughs rained the silvery lunar light like Christmas tassels.

Behind Longarm, a wildcat whined. At what? The Gunn and Cruz Bunch? Were they behind him? He couldn't tell. It had been dark for hours so he'd long ago given up looking for shadowers. He hadn't spied them before the sun had gone down, either, but Gunn and Cruz were sneaky. If they were near, he likely wouldn't know it.

He had to assume they were behind him, for he hadn't had time to cover his own tracks, let alone those

of the four gunmen who'd kidnapped Lacy. When
they'd reached the mountains, instead of swinging east
in the direction of the Arkansas River and Jawbone,
they'd headed west before turning north into the rugged slopes themselves. They'd followed a game path
up through the forested mountain shoulders, and Longarm had followed them, as the Gunn and Cruz Bunch
had probably followed him, and now here he was at
the edge of clearing somewhere in the craggy reaches
of the Sawatch Range.

Killers ahead of him, killers behind.

The wolf gave its mournful howl once more. The
short hairs lifted under Longarm's shirt collar. As he
stared out from the edge of the forest and into a broad
clearing beyond, he held his Winchester repeater
up high across his chest, index finger curled through
the trigger guard, his thumb worrying the uncocked
hammer.

On the far side of the clearing, a hundred yards
away, a cabin hunched at the base of another sheer
ridge that the moonlight painted nearly the white of
parchment. It was relieved in shadows. At the ridge's
rock-strewn base, Longarm could see the faint silver
line of what must have been a stream.

The cabin itself sat in front of the stream—a simple
log affair with a brush roof and a large hearth running
up the right end. Smoke gushed from the chimney,
unfurling like small, pale ghosts above the tops of the
pines that closed in around both sides of the cabin.
Longarm could see the vague shadow of a stable and
a corral flanking the cabin to the right.

The horses of Fallon, Brennan, Studemyer, and

Ryan were likely confined there. It had to be the gunmen and Lacy in the cabin. Their trail led directly out
from beneath Longarm's boots and into the clearing
toward the shack that had most likely been built by a
trapper or a prospector, for those were the only breed
of men who lived this far up in the craggy reaches.
Fallon or one of the other gunmen had to have known
about it previously, for their trail had led directly here
without wavering. The group had only stopped a few
times, quickly, to rest and water their horses.

And then they'd continued here—the four cold-steel
artists and their saucy prize.

Longarm stared at the shack's lighted windows.
They were likely in there at this very moment, enjoying what Dickie Shafter had enjoyed the night before.
Funny that Longarm couldn't hear her screaming,
though. Or maybe four at once was just her style . . .

His impulse was to hurry across the clearing and
save the girl, even though she didn't deserve it, but
caution was his friend. Most likely at least one of the
four gunmen was keeping scout over the place. They
had to have figured that Longarm was shadowing
them. He'd been surprised at least one of them hadn't
held back to bushwhack him earlier along the trail.

Leading the grullo into the forest left of the trace,
Longarm tied the reins around a low pine branch, then
unbuckled his saddle's belly strap and slipped the bridle bit from the animal's teeth, so it could blow and
forage. Longarm slipped his Winchester from its saddle sheath, quietly levered a cartridge into the chamber, off cocked the hammer, and strode slowly out of
the trees. He paused at the edge of the clearing, studying

the terrain around him, appraising the shack that was a purple shadow glazed with silver moonlight.

Ghostly puffs of smoke continued to rise from the hearth. Otherwise, there was no other movement the lawman could detect from this vantage.

He turned to his left and strode as quietly as possible along the edge of the clearing, staying close to the dark, towering pines whose silhouettes, he hoped, concealed his own. He resisted the urge to move more quickly. Getting himself shot by a hidden gunmen wasn't going to do Lacy Sackett any good . . .

It took him nearly twenty minutes to circle the clearing and to hunker down nearly directly behind the cabin. He could see it better now—at least its backside against which cut logs had been stacked. There was a privy, as well. He'd been right about the corral—it was off to his left. He could smell the horses on the cool, still air, hear one occasionally blowing or giving a soft nicker, probably having scented him.

The stream was no stream but a river. It was a good fifty yards across and bathed in moonlight, water flaring like silver stitches over and around rocks. There was a crude, flat-bottomed boat just behind Longarm, pulled up on shore and tied to a tree.

He stared over a boulder at the cabin. He couldn't tell if the gunmen had posted a scout. So far, he hadn't seen . . .

A shadow slipped around the cabin's right rear corner. He was stocky man wearing a black hat with a Texas crease in its crown. His gray deerskin vest had a copper stud in each flap, and two holsters were tied low on his thighs, gutta-percha-gripped Smith & Wessons jutting forward for the cross draw.

H. G. Ryan.

Longarm drew his head down behind the boulder, then, doffing his hat, edged a peek out around the left side. The gunman was holding a carbine up high across his chest. He kept his back close to the cabin and was looking around cautiously, sidestepping very slowly along the rear wall and the stacked logs toward the door in the cabin's center.

He must have heard something. When he got to the door he stopped in the depression worn in front of it. He stood there for a long time, holding the carbine and turning his head slowly from right to left and back again. He was bathed in silver and his shadow slanted back across the stacked wood and the cabin, the sashed windows of which were lit with a murky umber light.

Longarm waited, looking around him. There was only the murmuring stream bubbling over rocks. No breeze whatever. He and Ryan seemed to be the only two out here.

He glanced around the rock again. Ryan was still standing in front of the cabin. Had he spied him?

The gunman jerked his chin toward Longarm. Alarm bells tolled in the lawman's head, and he swung around just as a tall, slender shadow stepped out from a tree near the stream. Starlight flashed off the barrel of the rifle the man held to his shoulder. Longarm threw himself forward over his own feet at the same time that the rifle flashed brightly and thundered loudly in the heavy silence.

The slug hammered the boulder against which Long-arm had been sitting a half second before. As the man cursed and loudly racked another shell into the rifle's chamber, Longarm rolled onto his right hip, raised his own rifle, raking back the hammer, and fired once, twice, three times, the empty cartridge casings wing-ing back over his shoulder and clinking onto the gravel.

The tall man—Goose Fallon, most likely—flew back with a yell, triggering his rifle at the stars. As he hit the forest duff with a crunching thud, Longarm threw himself against the boulder again and snaked his rifle toward the cabin. He drew his head back when Ryan triggered two slugs into the ground around the boulder, blowing up dirt and gravel. Another slug loudly hammered the boulder, flinging stone shards.

There was a pause in the shooting, so Longarm snaked his rifle around the boulder's other side. Ryan stood there crouched, boots thudding and men yelling in the cabin behind him.

"Come out o' there, lawdog, and *maybe* we'll give you a turn with the girl!"

As the cabin door opened behind him, Longarm squeezed the Winchester's trigger. Ryan screamed and leaned forward, firing his carbine into the ground in front of him as he clutched his left knee, which Long-arm had just hammered with a .44-caliber slug. Long-arm fired again, higher, and Ryan fell back against the door frame as the door itself opened.

Longarm continued firing the Winchester through the open door until a grunt and a thud sounded.

He waited, staring through the wafting powder smoke. One man appeared to have fallen back inside the cabin. Ryan was hunkered down against the frame, groaning. Inside, the girl was screaming and a man was yelling raucously.

Longarm rose, flung his Winchester aside, as he figured he'd fired all nine rounds, then ran hard toward the cabin, palming his Colt and ratcheting back the hammer. He slowed as he approached the open door.

Ryan groaned, bleeding from the knee and his upper right chest. He slid his right hand toward one of his Smith & Wessons. Longarm kicked it out of his hand, then, spying movement inside the cabin, jerked back behind the cabin's back wall, right of the door, as a gun barked inside.

The slug chewed splinters from the door frame.

Longarm peeked around the frame as he snaked his Colt around it. Orrin Brennan knelt on the far side of a small table in the middle of the room, beneath a hanging lantern. The table was covered with playing cards, paper money and coins, smoldering half-smoked cigars, tin cups, and an uncorked whiskey bottle. Brennan grimaced, showing his large, yellow teeth beneath a dark brown mustache, and triggered his two Remingtons over the table. Longarm triggered his Colt at the same time, then winced as both of Brennan's bullets chewed into the door frame, spraying more splinters at him.

Longarm fired two more shots. Brennan cursed shrilly. Longarm bolted around the door frame and into the cabin. Ryan stood slumped against the far wall, beside a brass-framed bed upon which Lacy lay spread-eagled, her wrists and ankles bound to the frame. She was sobbing, turning her head toward the cabin's front wall on her right. Her naked breasts rose and fell heavily.

"Please, please, please!" she cried. "Stop! Stop! Please stop *shooting*!"

Orrin Brennan stood with his hair hanging low over his eyes, a grimace painted on his face, showing his yellow teeth. His left arm hung straight down at his side, limp from the bullet wound that bloodied his sleeve up near his shoulder. He held the pistol in his right hand against Lacy's head. He had his eyes on Longarm. A challenging grin quirked his mouth corners.

"Put down the shootin' iron, star packer, or I'll drill a hole through this nasty little bitch's purty *head*!"

Chapter 8

"Go ahead," Longarm said. "I'm right tired of her."

Longarm held his cocked Colt on Brennan's head, where the gunman's thin, dark brown hair had parted to reveal three veins forking above his nose. Brennan's lips stretched farther back from his mouth, revealing the gap of a missing tooth on one side.

"I'll do it! You think I won't, but I will! Now, drop that iron, Long, or I'll drill her a new ear!"

"No!" Lacy screamed at Longarm, straining against the ropes holding her spread-eagled on the mussed bed. "Longarm, please—he'll kill me."

"Nah, he won't," Longarm said, grinning. "Will you, Orrin?"

"I will! I swear I will!"

The gunman held his pistol taut against Lacy's head. Now he looked down at her, gritting his teeth. His eyes strayed down the length of her voluptuous form, taking in the jostling tits, furred snatch, and bending knees. He ground his teeth harder, till Longarm could hear them cracking. Brennan shifted his dire, frustrated gaze between Lacy to Longarm several times, Lacy sobbing and begging for her life, the bed squawking beneath her straining, naked form.

Finally, Brennan gave a raucous bellow of expressed vexation and swung his pistol toward Longarm. Before he could get the weapon steadied, Longarm's Colt barked three times quickly. Brennan slammed back against the wall, triggering his Remington wild, groaning and dropping his chin to look at the three holes lined up across his chest. Each one pumped blood out to dribble down his pin-striped shirt and brown leather vest.

"Ah, shit!" Brennan said as his knees buckled.

He hit the floor with a thud and fell forward on his face. He wagged his head as though he couldn't believe what had just happened, and then he lay still.

Lacy screamed. Longarm wheeled, following the girl's anxious gaze, to see Studemyer bringing a pistol up from the floor where a good half of his blood must have leaked out. His pistol roared a half second before Longarm's pistol followed suit, hammering a quarter-sized hole through the middle of the man's forehead. As Studemyer slammed back against the floor, into his own molasses-thick blood pool, Longarm winced at the icy-hot slice across his left side. He touched his hand to it, felt the greasy slickness of blood.

Just a burn. He'd tend it later.

He turned to the girl, who lay back against a pillow, sobbing. "Cut me loose. Oh, please cut me loose, Longarm. Those brigands! Did you see what they did to Dickie?"

"I saw."

He took out his folding knife and cut the ropes, freeing her wrists and ankles. She rolled toward Longarm, dropping her bare legs over the side of the bed and wrapping her arms around his waist, burying her face in his belly.

"Thank you for coming after me! I didn't think you would. I really didn't think you would!"

"Oh, I got a feelin' you did."

He stared straight down at her, trying to ignore the push of her breasts against his groin. He couldn't help asking, "Did they . . . ?"

She shook her head slightly, making his cock tingle. "They were playing poker for me. Winner was to have the first *turn*!" She sobbed, quivering against him and increasing his discomfort. "Oh, what *savages*!"

"Hey," said H. G. Ryan, still crouched against the outside of the door frame, looking in. His voice was slurred, pinched with pain. "I'm in agony over here."

Ignoring the wounded gunman, Longarm leaned down and drew a wool blanket over Lacy's shoulders. "You'd best get some clothes . . ."

He let his voice trail off, cocking his head to listen. He'd heard something. He heard it again—a horse nickering in the corral. As he walked to the door, he flicked open the Colt's loading gate, shook the empty shell casings onto the floor, and began refilling the chambers from his cartridge belt.

He opened the door slowly, listened through the crack.

"What is it?" Lacy whispered, stumbling around dressing.

"Stay here. Don't poke your fool head outside 'less you want it shot off."

"Oh, God—it's Gunn and Cruz, isn't it?"

"I said shut up!"

"Fuck you, you bastard!" she whispered.

"I'm dyin' over here," Ryan said in a low, mild voice. "If anyone cares . . ."

"Keep him quiet, too," Longarm told Lacy. "If you have to beat him over the head with a log."

Longarm opened the door wider and stepped out quickly. Drawing the door closed behind him, he put his back to the cabin wall right of it, hoping the wall's shadow concealed him. He stood there looking around and listening for several minutes, hearing nothing more than a couple of the gunmen's horses nickering and milling inside their corral.

Cautiously, Longarm moved out away from the cabin and started walking across the clearing. The moon had angled off behind the mountains to the west, and the clearing was dark. He held his Colt straight out in front of him, wishing he had his rifle, wondering if Gunn's men were out here somewhere, maybe surrounding the cabin.

If they were, they were damn quiet.

Twice he paused and dropped to a knee, tension rippling up and down his spine as he looked around carefully. Both times, however, he decided that it had been some burrowing creature rattling dead leaves and brush in the black forest around him that had stopped him.

When he reached the edge of the forest, he continued into the gap in the trees that marked where the

trail entered the clearing, and found his grullo standing where he'd left it. But the horse's tail was arched
slightly, and it was twitching its ears. As he walked
up, the horse lurched with a start and whinnied.

"Shhh!" Longarm said, grabbing the bridle and placing a calming hand on the horse's sleek neck. "Easy,
boy. Easy!"

He slipped the bit back into the horse's mouth, then
buckled the belly strap. That seemed to settle the horse
some. It stood, raking air in and out of its big lungs
like a bellows, and its eyes were shiny, but it didn't
look like it was going to kick up another fuss, so Longarm stepped away from it quietly. He moved back out
to the trail he'd followed here. In the shadow of a tam-
arack, he stood still, looking around, pricking his ears.

His breath jetted from his nostrils, waftng like
smoke in the frosty air.

There was a flash from the darkness off the trail's
opposite side and at a slightly higher elevation. As the
slug slammed into the tree about six inches above Longarm's head, the gun's clap reached his ears, echoing
flatly between the ridges. He jerked into a crouch and
automatically triggered the Colt at the place where
he'd seen the gun flash.

Knowing the shooters would aim at his own flashes,
he stepped sideways, fired twice more, then, as several
more guns flashed and popped from the other side of
the trail, he dove sideways and rolled behind a fir.

"Hey, lawdog—that you?" a man yelled when the
shooting dropped off.

Longarm waited, breathing hard as he shoved fresh
brass through his Colt's loading gate.

"This is Heck Gunn. You send that double-crossing little bitch out here, and we'll let you go—got it?" the man yelled.

Longarm paused for a split second, then punched the last cartridge into his pistol and spun the cylinder. "I don't get it," Longarm yelled. "How'd she double-cross you, Heck?"

A pause.

"She knows how," Gunn said darkly.

Longarm thought about that. The statement didn't surprise him, but he couldn't help wondering how—in what sordid way—did Lacy double-cross the crooked bunch she'd thrown in with back in Jawbone. Slowly, he began to step straight back away from the fir, keeping his Colt extended, intending to get back to the grullo and hightail it for the cabin.

"Hey, lawdog," another man said, this one with a Spanish accent. "You hear *mi* amigo, Heck—no? You send the blond *puta* out here, we let you live. You don't, we come and get her and kill you slow, cut your ears and balls off and fry them up together in a hot skillet while you watch."

Forbidding, disembodied chuckles rose from the forest's inky darkness.

That last made Longarm wince. Damn, he thought, these boys were really sore at the girl. Again, he wondered just what in the hell she'd done to chafe these hard cases so badly that they'd come this far for her. He'd thought they'd turned back from their run to Mexico because they, like himself, rather enjoyed how she looked and performed without her clothes on.

But, no—somehow she'd planted a bee under their

saddle blankets, as she had his own, and they were out to give the devil her due.

Longarm doubted threats would work, but why not give it a shot? As he backed toward his horse, putting one foot down carefully after another, he said, "You're messin' with holy fire here, fellas. I'm Custis Long, deputy United States marshal out of Denver. Lacy Sackett is my prisoner, and—"

"Longarm?" one of the voices interrupted him.

"That's right."

"Hey, I heard o' you!" another owlhoot said.

"Then you know I don't fool around. So, lessen you wanna hang—"

He was interrupted this time by a raucous, mocking howl accompanied by rifle and pistol fire. The guns flashed in the darkness, the bullets screeching around the lawman and chewing into tree boles and clipping branches.

So much for trying to reason with old Heck Gunn and Orlando Cruz, Longarm thought as he lunged for his crow-footing grullo. He tripped over a slender, fallen tree but managed to hoist himself into the saddle and rip his reins free as the horse gave a shrill whinny and turned toward the north, away from the gunfire.

"Hi-yahh!" Longarm grated out beneath the crackling of the Gunn and Cruz gang's fusillade, crouching low in the saddle and ramming his heels hard against the grullo's flanks.

The horse buck-kicked and galloped on through the trees, bulling through the thick scrub. Bullets slammed into the trees around it and Longarm, one burning across the top of his left shoulder and making him wince. As the horse bulled into the clearing, it hesitated, screaming and pitching, and Longarm gripped the apple as he twisted around and fired three shots back in the direction from which he'd come.

Then he rammed his heels hard once more against the grullo's flanks, and horse and rider lunged toward the cabin lights glowing weakly on the other side of the clearing. Hunkered low and gritting his teeth, the gunfire softening behind him, Longarm turned the horse slightly right and left, making a zigzag pattern in an attempt to outrun the gang's flying lead.

Finally, the gunfire dwindled to only one or two shots before dying altogether. Longarm checked the grullo down in front of the cabin, swung down, grabbed his saddlebags and bedroll off its back, and pushed through the cabin's door.

He stopped in the open doorway. Lacy stood before him, dressed in a heavy coat over her torn gray shirt and long skirt, and in a man's battered Stetson, aiming a big Remington at him. The gun was cocked. Her hands were shaking.

"Nooo!" she screamed as, closing her eyes and turning her face away from the gun, it leaped and roared in her hands, its kick sending her stumbling straight backward.

Longarm had thrown himself hard left against the door as the girl's bullet careened through the opening behind him. Pushing off the door frame, he hurled himself forward and onto the girl, turning to one side before they hit the floor together, Longarm ripping the Remington from her slender hands.

"What the hell you think you're doing, you damn crazy catamount?" he bellowed.

She lay on her side, hair hanging down across her face, gasping and peering at him wide-eyed through the honey-blond locks. "I thought you were *them!*" she screamed, throwing herself against him.

Her sudden weight sent him onto his back with Lacy squirming around on top of him, wrapping her arms around his neck and pressing her head to his chest. Even through his coat and her coat, he could feel the swell of her breasts against him, was visited with another vague, ludicrous pang of desire.

"Get off me, goddamnit!" he barked. "We don't have time for no tearful reunions. Gunn and Cruz are behind me, probably headed this way, angry as hornets." Rising, peering outside carefully, not liking the eerie silence hanging heavy as an August storm over the clearing, he pulled his saddlebags and bedroll inside and kicked the door closed.

Turning to her, confused thoughts tumbling around inside his head, he said, "Say, what the hell did you do to get them boys' necks in such a hump, anyway?"

She lay propped on her elbows, and a faint flush rose in her tapered cheeks. "What did they say?"

Hoof thuds rose outside the cabin. Longarm opened the door and edged a look through the crack. Jostling shadows were moving toward him from the clearing's far side—a good ten or so riders, their tack flashing in the starlight. There were too many for him to hold off even from inside the cabin.

Gunn and Cruz would either shoot him out or burn him out.

"Never mind." He closed and barred the door, then slung his saddlebags over one shoulder, clamped his bedroll under his arm, and jerked her to her feet. "Come on—we're gonna have to light a shuck."

"Where to?"

"As far as I can tell, there's only one way out of this canyon that ain't via the river, and Gunn and Cruz done have that trail covered."

"So . . . ?"

He grabbed a small sack of what appeared to be food off a shelf, shoved it against her chest, then pushed her toward the back door. "So, we're gonna have to light off down stream. Go!"

He'd followed her out the back door when he turned toward H. G. Ryan, whose legs he'd nearly tripped over. The gunman was no longer leaning against the door frame. He lay on his side. Blood oozed in two rivulets down the side of his head from just over his ear. He wasn't moving. A stick of bloodstained stove wood lay near his head.

Longarm looked at Lacy, who had turned to give him a sheepish look.

"You told me to keep him quiet!" she cried. "Now, just with the hell are you talking about—how are we going to get downstream?"

"Ain't that what boats are usually for?"

Longarm brushed past her, picked up his rifle from where he'd left it near the boulder, and strode over to the boat that hunched in the shadows of a tall willow at the edge of the water. The girl was running along behind him. He couldn't hear the hoof thuds of Gunn and Cruz from here, because of the stream, but he was sure they were working their way around the cabin, likely assuming that he and the girl were still inside.

They'd know soon enough that they weren't.

"I'm not getting on that thing," Lacy said as Longarm set his gear in the boat. A paddle lay across the two log seats.

"That's up to you." Longarm had untied the boat's rope from a branch of the willow and tossed it aboard, then began shoving the rickety vessel out into the water beyond a gently slanting shelf of scalloped sand. "But if I was you, with as mad as you seem to have made your ole pards Gunn and Cruz, I'd reconsider."

Longarm kicked the boat into deeper water, until it started bobbing and slowly turning downstream. Guns barked and flashed from the direction of the cabin. The slugs blew up dirt and gravel along the shore of the river, one within inches of Lacy's right foot.

"Wait!" she called, running into the stream. "Oh, Longarm—wait for *me*!"

Chapter 9

As the bullets ripped up the water around Lacy, one thudding into the boat near Longarm's right knee, he reached out and grabbed her hand. She screamed as another bullet blew up water beside her, and then he pulled her up out of the knee-deep water and into the boat. He extended the paddle out over the boat's opposite, trying to equally distribute their weight so they wouldn't swamp.

While the girl folded up on the rough planks between the two seats, Longarm picked up his Winchester, quickly plucked shells from his cartridge belt, and thumbed them through the rifle's loading gate. The boat bobbed and weaved, bouncing off rocks.

"Oh, God!" the girl cried, burying her head in her arms. "We're doomed. *Doomed!*"

As Longarm saw the shadows of several men running toward the river from the cabin, their guns flashing,

ricochets screeching off rocks and slapping the water
around him, he dropped to a knee and raised the Winchester.

Bam! Bam! Bam! Bam! Bam!

He heard a yelp that was nearly inaudible above the
river's quiet rush, the occasional thuds of the boat
bouncing off rocks, and the girl's sobbing. The other
shadows dropped, and the rifles and pistols flashed
again as Gunn's men kept up their fusillade.

"Doomed!" Lacy cried. "Oh, damnit, I had such
big plans!"

But then suddenly the boat drifted behind a screen
of brush and spindly trees, and then a mountain wall
slid past on Longarm's right, and the gun flashes disappeared, as did the screeching and slapping of the
gang's angry bullets. The boat pitched sharply to the
right, and Longarm nearly flew out of it. He dropped
to a knee and steadied himself on the gunwale.

Looking around at the dark, silver water around
him, he saw that they were in the middle of the stream
though still bouncing off rocks, tossing and turning.
Just then, a corner of the boat went over a large rock
firmly planted on the river's bottom, and Lacy screeched
as she rolled toward the opposite side of the boat. Longarm grabbed her just before she would have tumbled
overboard.

"Hold on!" he shouted.

Setting his rifle down, he picked up the paddle.
With effort, he got the boat turned so that the prow
was heading downstream. They dropped over a slight
falls and then the river widened between towering,

black ridges and became more placid. The boat slid smoothly off through the easy ripples between rocks.

The ridges were steep on both sides. The river was as black as the inside of a glove. Eerily black with only the occasional flash of ambient light off a wavelet. The water gurgled against the sides of the boat. That was the only sound. Even Lacy had fallen silent under the river's hushed influence.

After they'd drifted around a slight bend, she whispered, "It's so dark I can't see a thing."

"Yeah," Longarm said, trying to keep the boat in the middle of the stream though there were damn few reference points to tell him where the middle was.

The river chugged quietly. Wolves howled in the mountains. A night bird cooed.

The boat drifted quietly, moving at what Longarm figured was only about three or four miles an hour— about walking speed. He kept his ear pricked for the thud of horse hooves. He hadn't gotten a good enough look at the clearing to know if any trails led out of it along the stream. He hoped not. Or, if there were trails, he hoped that Gunn and Cruz didn't find them, which didn't seem likely as dark as it was out here.

"How far we gonna go?" Lacy asked, her quiet voice sounding crisp and inordinately loud in the heavy silence.

Longarm used a handkerchief to dab at the bullet burn along his side. "Not sure. For a time."

"Used to driving a boat, are you?"

"Nope."

"Oh, God, what if there's a falls?" Lacy's voice rose

with anxiety. "What if there's a falls ahead and we can't see it because it's so goddamn dark?"

"They teach you that blue tongue of yours back home in the piano parlor, did they?"

Longarm's wry tone belied his own fear of the same thing. He didn't recognize this part of the Sawatch in the dark, but he was beginning to think they were on the Mulehead River, a relatively short stream but one that threaded through several deep canyons in the Sawatch before emptying out in the Arkansas farther east. If the Mulehead indeed was the river he was on, he'd have his work cut out for him, as he'd heard there were several nasty stretches where the river dropped fast. Those stretches would likely be worse this time of the year, when the low water would expose more rocks like the one they'd gone over and that had nearly capsized them.

He heard Lacy's teeth clattering. It was so dark that he couldn't see much of her but the light tan of her coat and hat, the blond of her hair. Her breath shone in the air around her head. It was cold out here, and she'd likely caught a good chill running through the water.

Longarm adjusted their coarse with the paddle and cursed.

"What is it?" she said, looking around fearfully as though expecting to see Gunn and Cruz bearing down on them from the pale cliff faces on either side of the trail.

"You."

"What about me?"

"We're gonna have to stop soon or you'll catch your death of cold."

Her teeth continued to clatter, and her voice shook as she said. "No! We mustn't stop yet, Longarm. What if Heck catches up to us?"

Longarm gave a wry snort and studied her vague form in the darkness just ahead of him and left. "Maybe I should let 'em catch up to us. Turn you over to 'em. Why the hell not? Why take you back to Jawbone to stand trial when it looks like Gunn and Cruz have a better idea?"

She jerked her head toward him so quickly that she nearly lost her hat. "No!"

She softened her voice, made it silky and alluring so that whomever heard it would think about other things that were sexy about her.

"You wouldn't, would you, Longarm? They're awful men. Truly they are. I realize now how mistaken I was to hook up with them." She paused, raked a liquid sigh as though she were about to tear up. "You see, I was just so bored at home. And Dickie . . . well, he was a nice enough fellow, but I just couldn't stand the thought of living out there on that big ranch so far from town. Him and his father . . . hell . . . I mean, heck . . . they would have turned me into their slave."

Her voice became crisper, as though she couldn't keep up the charade long without the real Lacy Sackett resurfacing. "Old Ezekial is rich enough to buy and sell all of Colorado Territory, but he's so cheap he won't even hire a housekeeper. That's the real reason he wanted Dickie to marry me. That and the fact that my father owns the bank in Jawbone. The old bastard said I had good, childbearing hips, and I looked strong enough to keep up a house!"

"I take it you didn't shed too many tears over ole Dickie after Goose and the other gut-shot him and left him layin' along the trail to die, eh?"

"Goddamn you! You just won't listen to me, will you?"

Longarm looked at her. Even knowing how devilish she was, her anger still startled him. It had to come from somewhere other than that lovely face and body of hers. It had to belong to a demon inside her.

"How'd you rub Gunn and Cruz so raw?" he asked her, hearing her teeth chatter. Apparently, her rage hadn't warmed her any.

Lacy stared at him but didn't say anything for several seconds. Then she hugged herself: "If you stop and build a fire to get me dry and warm, I'll tell you."

Longarm watched her. He'd rarely been afraid of women—at least, women not aiming a gun at him—but this girl constantly made him feel as though he were staring down the deep, black maw of a cocked derringer.

What did she have up her sleeve? Or did she really just want him to stop and build a fire?

"Thought you were afraid they'd catch up to us."

"We've come far enough now. They'll never find us in the darkness. I doubt there's even any trails back in those mountains. Besides, I know you'll protect me, Custis."

Longarm snorted at how deep and sultry her voice had gone with that last sentence. He sighed but started looking around for a place to land the boat. The cliff walls continued to bulge up close to the river for another mile or so, then fell back. Especially the one

on the north side. Longarm brought the boat closer to
that side of the river and saw a wide area of relatively
flat shoreline. Quickly, fighting the current, he dug the
paddle into the river and swung the boat's nose toward
shore.

When the boat scraped the bottom and gave a shudder, he set the paddle down and leaped off the boat
and into the river, the water here climbing to his knees
and causing him to suck a sharp breath against the
chill. Snow must still have been melting in the high
country, as it had been a relatively cool summer.

He pulled the boat to shore with the rope, helped
Lacy off, then tied the rope around a small tree about
ten feet away from the water. Looking around, he scrutinized the flat around him. The north ridge fell back
far enough to let some starlight in, so he could see better here than he had been a little ways upriver.

"Come on," he said, grabbing his saddlebags, bedroll, and rifle. He'd spied a notch between steep ridges,
and he headed for the black crack now, the girl following him and audibly shivering.

A few minutes later, he found a notch cave deep
inside the crack, well hidden from the river. By the
light of a torch he made from a chunk of dry driftwood
and a lucifer, he gathered wood and built a small fire
inside the cave. Both he and Lacy hunkered over the
fledgling flames, rubbing their hands and warming
themselves.

When the fire had grown a bit, spreading a comfort-
ing warmth inside the small, rocky cavern, Lacy
quickly shed her coat. She didn't stop there. Off came
Dickie's shirt and then her chemise. Bare breasts

jiggling, she turned onto her rump and slid her skirt
and pantaloons down her legs, until she sat before him,
knees slightly raised, arms crossed beneath her pale
breasts, shivering and favoring Longarm with that sexy
jade gaze of hers.

"Oh, what I wouldn't give for some hot water for a
sponge bath!" She leaned forward, wrapping her arms
around her legs. Her breasts sloped forward, away
from her chest, until she pressed them against her
knees, blinking at him and coyly smiling.

His cock tingled and his loins itched.

"Ah, shit." He picked up his tin pot, coffeepot, and
his rifle, looking around to make sure there were no
other weapons she could get a hold of. Seeing nothing
more than rocks, but reminding himself that she could
make good use of those if she wanted, he pinned her
with a commanding look. "You stay here and behave
yourself."

"You're a wonderful man, Custis Long!" she yelled
back at him as he crouched out of the cave to fetch
water from the river.

He grumbled a reply and headed down the uneven
cleft in the rocks, trailing a hand along the rock wall
on his left, the starlight dimly lighting his way. When
he got to the river, he dragged the boat into some
brush, where it would be less conspicuous if Gunn and
Cruz found a way into this wilderness. Then he filled
both pots, and grumbling his frustration over the girl
once more—one second he wanted nothing more than
to throw her down and take her, the next he wanted
nothing but to drill a bullet through her pretty head—
he strode back to the cave.

Cautiously, he glanced inside the cavern, making sure she wasn't about to try to brain him again with a rock. She was lounging on the same side of the fire as before, only now she was facing the entrance.

She had her knees bent slightly, and she sat propped on her outstretched arms, head thrown back, pointing those beautiful, firm, upturned orbs at the cave ceiling on which the fire danced redly. It danced redly on her body, as well, lending her the aspect of a demon dancing in the fires of hell—albeit a beautiful, willowy, curvy demon with honey-blond hair.

As he ducked into the cave, his rifle under his arm, she looked at him and smiled beautifully, jade eyes flashing. "Thank you!"

He grumbled another reply, set both pots near the flames, then sat back against the cave wall and reached into his buckskin to dig a three-for-a-nickel cheroot from the breast pocket of his frock coat. He struck a match, got the smoke going, and stared at the egg-shaped cave opening as he said, "Let's have it."

"Let's have what?" In the periphery of his vision, he saw her looking at him with wide-eyed innocence. Then her eyelids dropped halfway and her mouth corners rose lustily. "Are you saying you'd like me again, Longarm? Maybe you've been thinking about how much fun we had, and you'd like to impale me again with that ax handle of yours."

She shrugged. "I know I certainly wouldn't mind it a bit. Might even take my mind off all the trouble I'm in!"

Chapter 10

"What I want to know," Longarm said, trying to ignore her taunting invitation, staring out the oval-shaped cavern door, puffing the cheroot with a little too much vigor, "is what kind of trouble you got yourself into with Gunn and Cruz?"

"Do you have something I can wash myself with?"

Frowning, he turned to where she still sprawled as though on some red plush settee in an expensive flesh parlor in Denver, naked as the day she was born. He let smoke dribble out his nostrils. "Huh?"

"I asked you if you have something I could wash myself with, Longarm."

He gave another disgusted chuff. "Reach into my saddlebags there."

She leaned over, flattening one leg while tilting the other toward it, and rummaged around in one of his saddlebag pouches. She pulled a frayed green cloth he used for giving himself the occasional whore's bath when out on the trail, and a cake of lye soap tucked inside it, then pulled the steaming cook pot to the side of the fire. She rose up onto her knees, soaked the cloth in the water, wrung it out, and rubbed the soap over it.

Slowly, gently, she began rubbing the rag down her right arm while Longarm pointedly ignored her, knowing she wanted nothing more than to get him worked up so he'd forget the question and maybe even forget about hauling her beautiful, nasty ass back to Jawbone.

"Would you like to do this for me?" she asked, staring at him from beneath her brow on the other side of the fire, the flames playing beguilingly over her breasts, shoulders, flat belly, swelling hips, and long, supple thighs. It caused copper sparks to flick like miniature javelins from her eyes.

He couldn't help feasting his eyes on her hands and the soapy rag and the breast she was soaping so thoroughly, the nipple jouncing as she did. He swallowed down the hard knot in his throat, grunted softly at the pull of his pants across his stiffening member.

"I'll say I don't," he said, hearing the lie in his own heavy words. "But you go ahead and take your time. We got all night, I reckon."

"Oh, you're such a sourpuss!" she said, pooching her lips out in a pout. "Okay, if you must know, I snuck off away from the camp you found me in . . . with the money that Heck Gunn and Orlando Cruz stole from my father's bank."

She lifted her chin and closed her eyes in sensual delight as she ran the wet, soapy cloth up over her right breast, making it jiggle. As the import of what she'd just said reached his brain, he lifted his eyes from the soapy orb to her eyes on the other side of the fire.

Lines of incredulity sawed across his forehead. "You what?"

She giggled and gently squeezed the soapy nipple between her thumb and index finger, causing it to stiffen. "Sure enough. I double-crossed them before they had time to double-cross me. You don't think they'd really take me all the way to Mexico with them, do you? When men like that get their fill of a girl, they toss her out like the bacon rinds on a trash heap."

She continued to pinch the pebbling nipple while running the soapy cloth over her other breast. "That's what I was off doing when you found me. I'd just finished burying the money bag where they wouldn't find it."

"What about the men I had to shoot two nights ago?"

"Oh, them." Lacy chuckled. "Me and those three had a double-cross on. I was to sneak away from the camp with the loot and hide it and then meet up with them later, after they'd bushwhacked the others. You sort of tied a knot on our plans, Longarm—at least the part about me running away and meeting up with the others later to retrieve the loot. I figured I'd need those three to get me safely to San Francisco, you see."

Longarm sat riveted, his back pressed taut against the cave wall. He lifted the half-smoked cheroot to his lips once more, drew the smoke deep into his lungs, and let it out slowly, thinking over what she'd told him while unable to stop watching her hands massage her breasts.

It was like having a whole hive of angry bees buzz-
ing around in his head. He couldn't think straight. His
pants and balbriggans were drawn taut across his
groin, his rock-hard cock throbbing, wanting nothing
so badly as to burst free of its confines and have its
way with the exquisitely intoxicating witch bathing on
the other side of the fire. Her own eyes were on his midsection. Those copper, green-ensconced light javelins
caressed him as would her warm, soft fingers, and he
couldn't help imagining, with one part of his brain,
those fingers stroking him, as with the rest of his mind
he tried to sort through what she'd divulged.

Christ, she had a hold on him. Just as she had a
vice-like hold on every other man she came across. It
was every bit as unsettling as it was arousing!

"You took the money," he said tonelessly, narrow-
ing his eyes as he took another drag off the cheroot,
unconsciously trying to clear his mind with the smoke,
"and buried it . . ."

"Correct."

She continued to stare at him as she very slowly
rinsed the soap off her breasts. She dried herself with
his blanket, then spread it out beside her, right up close
to the fire, and lay down upon it. She turned on her
side facing him, head propped on an elbow. She
crooked her finger at him, her lips spread to show the
glistening white line of her teeth.

"Now, come over here, Longarm."

"Uh-uh," he grunted.

"I know you want to."

"Nope, I ain't gonna do that." Longarm felt drunk
though he hadn't had a shot of rye for a long time. His

coffee water was boiling, but he was only vaguely aware of it. "You're bad, Lacy. You're about as bad as they come, and I ain't . . ."

She opened her legs slightly. The firelight shone on the pink petals of the flower at her center, beneath her belly button. The silky, blond fur there shone wetly, as did the pink flesh nestling inside it.

Inside the pink was a small, dark line that was her opening. Slowly, she dropped her hand to it, touched her index finger to the opening.

"Come on over here, Longarm. You don't want me to have to do this all by myself, do you?"

With her other hand, she cupped her breast, slowly massaged it.

"Christ." Longarm flicked his cigar into the fire. Why fight it? He wouldn't be able to think straight until he had her again. Maybe after one more time, he'd finally have her out of his system.

He was thinking like an addict and he knew it. Still, he found himself climbing to his feet, kicking out of his boots, unbuckling his gun belt, and shucking out of all his clothes except his balbriggans. He walked over to her, lay down beside her. She rolled toward him, kissed him hungrily, and massaged his cock through his balbriggans.

She pulled her lips back from his, looked down at his cock that appeared a giant blood sausage pushing out from behind the crotch of his threadbare under-wear, slanting up against his thigh, throbbing. It was so hard that the big mushroom head was clearly defined.

She ran her small hand across it, staring at it, while

he nuzzled her left breast and massaging the other one, cupping it, hefting it gently, flicking his thumb across the nipple. Fires of raging desire burned within him. Everything else went away in his mind except the warmth of her, the touch of her, the feel of her damp, warm breast in his hand . . . the smoothness of her neck beneath his mustache as he nuzzled it . . .

"Take it out, Longarm," she said. "Take it out and let me suck it."

"Ah, Christ."

"Take it out," she whispered in a commanding tone. "Oh, never mind," she said, her voice sharp and somehow even more alluring. "I'll do it myself!" She shoved both hands inside his balbriggans, widening the fly with one hand while pulling his long, throbbing member out with the other.

"I was thinking about this when Dickie was fucking me," she whispered, holding the base of it in both hands, staring down at its long, thick, throbbing length jutting up over his belly button. "I was thinking about how much more fun I'd be having if it were you fucking me from behind, like Dickie was doing in his inept little way . . ."

She pumped him so hard with both hands, gritting her teeth, that it almost hurt. But what exquisite pain! Longarm lay back on his elbows and watched her hands work their hard magic.

She turned her hands this way and that, grunting softly with the effort. Finally, she lowered her head and went to work on him with her mouth nearly as vigorously as with her hand, her loud sucking and moaning sounds filling the small, firelit cavern.

Longarm squeezed his eyes shut and curled his toes. "Ah, bless me," he groaned, all thoughts of Gunn and Cruz and the money and Lacy's wickedness shuffling off to the far, dark reaches of his brain.

It was only her in his mind now. Her and her lips. Her tongue. Her breasts raking his thighs, her hair lightly caressing his belly and balls as she sucked him.

"'Nough o' that," he said through a groan, when he couldn't stand it any longer, the juices fairly exploding out of him. "Time to finish proper."

He pushed her onto her back, but as he started to mount her, she squirmed around on her belly. "No, like this. The way I imagined you were doing it when Dickie was sticking his little thing in me."

"Fine as frog hair."

She climbed to her hands and knees, looked over her shoulder at him, and wagged her pretty, pale ass that was burnished salmon by the firelight. She giggled, then, as he hunched over her, reaching around her to cup her breasts in his hands, she reached down past her belly, wrapped her hand around his cock, and guided the head through her portal.

She sighed, whimpered. Longarm grunted, feeling her wet heat and the flesh just inside her tender as molasses in a warm jar. He pushed his rod farther in.

"Wait, wait!" she said, lifting her head, her rich hair tumbling down to the slender small of her back. "Oh, God . . . wait! Okay, now . . . just a little at a time or you'll split me wide open!"

Longarm curled his lip with own brand of devilishness. He adjusted his knees, grabbed each tit harder, squeezing, and rammed the entire length of his shaft deep inside her, until he thought he could feel her heart hammering against the swollen head.

"Ahhhh!" she cried, the scream echoing shrilly around the cavern. "Oh, God, you fucking *bass-tard*! Don't you dare stop, damn you. Fuck me! Fuck me good, Longarm. I've been a very bad girl, and I deserve it hard and nasty . . . oh, Jesus *Chri-iist*!"

He hammered against her wildly, his groin slapping loudly against her ass. She sobbed and groaned and cried out for mercy, then berated him to fuck her harder, as hard as he could. "And don't come too fast, you bastard, because I've never known it could be like this and I want it to last forever!"

But when he could feel that she was ready by the frantic contracting of her pussy against him and the intensifying of her heat and wetness, he let go with a guttural roar of his own, tipping his head far back and hearing his own bearlike love cry reverberating around the cavern like empty barrels bouncing around in a freight wagon.

He drove nearly literally right into the ground.

When he finished, he pulled out of her, his cock still dripping on her pink ass, and she lay belly down on the blanket, arms thrown straight up above her head, groaning.

He rolled onto his back beside her. They were both breathing as hard as a couple of Pony Express horses.

When Lacy finally caught hers, she rolled onto her back beside him, dropped one hand to his dwindled cock, and said, "Oh, Custis, it could be like this every night . . . every morning . . . hell, it could be like this every hour of every day! . . . if we dug up the bank loot and ran off together. Just you and me and thirty-some dollars!"

He drew a deep breath, felt his heart slowing.

"What do you say, Custis?" She tickled his balls with the tips of her fingers.

"I say forget it."

Silence.

She pulled her hand away from his balls. A second later he saw the hand arcing toward him from his left. It was a fist now, and the fist had a stout chunk of wood in it. Longarm grabbed the wrist a foot above his head and pressed the barrel of his Colt against her forehead.

She stared down at him, her mouth open wide, eyes cast with horror.

He ratcheted the Colt's hammer back loudly. "Let's get it straight, you saucy little wench," he snarled through gritted teeth. "I don't care how many times you lure me between those beautiful legs of yours. You're going to lead me to that loot or I'm going to drill a .44 round through your purty head and toss your hot little carcass to the *wildcats*! You clear on that?"

Chapter 11

Longarm made the troublesome Lacy Sackett sleep handcuffed so he could saw a few logs himself.

He needed it. The night before, when he and the gunmen had lay listening to her pleasing the dear departed Dickie Shafter, seemed a lifetime ago. He woke sometime before dawn, the girl sleeping curled against him for warmth, as, since he'd been too busy frolicking with his prisoner, he hadn't been able to gather much wood for a fire. He blew the coals back to life, tossed the rest of the wood on the fire, and thought through his situation.

As soon as he could find a couple of horses, he'd take Lacy to where the loot was buried. He probably wouldn't kill her if she refused to tell him the stolen money's exact location, but it made him feel better to tell himself he would. And he thought he had her convinced that he would, too. What he'd seen in her eyes

when he'd snugged the butt of his Colt to her head had
been genuine terror.

"You're a damn fool," she said later that morning,
as he hauled his gear back out to the boat. She followed
close on his heels, hands cuffed behind her back so
she couldn't try to brain him again. "No man in his
right mind would turn down that much money, not to
mention a girl like me. Not only one as beautiful as I
am, but one who can please a man like I can. *Fool!*"

"Don't forget the great personality," Longarm said,
chuckling, as he dropped his gear on the boat. "That's
an added benefit."

"A girl doesn't need a personality when she's got
the other stuff."

"I don't know—a good ride between the sheets goes
only so far when the rest of the time a man's gotta listen to all that caterwaulin'. And sleep with one eye
open."

"Shut up, Longarm! Just shut up!"

"Took the words out of my mouth," he said, tossing
the rope onto the boat and kicking the boat into the
water that was gray-green in the cool dawn. He went
over and removed her handcuffs, stuffed them into his
coat pocket. "Now, get aboard or I'll leave you here
for Gunn and Cruz."

"Fuck Gunn and Cruz!"

"You already done that and look where it got you."
He gave her a brusque shove and she stumbled into the
boat, nearly overturning it. She squealed. Longarm
grabbed the side and steadied it before giving it
another, harder shove and leaping inside.

Lacy shuffled to the front of the boat and sat down,

facing him, hunched over with her elbows on her knees. As he paddled them into the middle of the river where there didn't seem to be so many rocks, she said, "Think about it, will you? Just think about it?"

"All right, I'll think about it," he lied.

He just wanted her to shut up.

When the boat was drifting steadily between the gradually lightening cliffs, he sat down and used the paddle only to adjust their course. The current moved them along at a slow jog. Where it would take them, he had no idea. But he hoped they'd come upon a ranch or settlement somewhere along the stream, so he could appropriate a mount, saddle up, and ride off to retrieve the Jawbone loot.

As the sky continued lightening and the ridges pulled back away from the stream, Longarm carefully scrutinized both shores. He'd seen a trail angling down a northern bluff, which meant Gunn and Cruz might be on the prowl, maybe even holed up along the stream somewhere to effect an ambush.

Last night, before Lacy had confessed absconding with the Jawbone loot, Longarm had figured there was a good possibility that Gunn and Cruz would decide there were probably plenty of good-looking gals along the trail to Mexico. They'd decide that one Miss Lacy Sackett, despite being likely the greatest tumble on earth, was just too damn much trouble, so they'd stop stalking her and Longarm and head back south.

He doubted that now. In fact, he knew they wouldn't leave the loot.

He fired a lucifer on his thumbnail, touched it to a fresh cheroot, and scrutinized a small stand of willows along the stream's southern shore. No, they were out here. And sooner or later, he'd run into them . . .

An hour later, the sun cleared the ridges and rained liquid gold onto the stream and the leaves of the ponderosa pines, willows, and aspens along both shores. Some fish jumped near a dead, bark-less pine tree that extended partway out from the northern shore. Water splashed near the boat, also. It made a hollow chugging sound.

The flat report of a rifle reached Longarm's ears half a second later. Longarm saw the black-hatted rifleman with a red neckerchief kneeling behind the fallen tree, levering another round into his Winchester's breech. At the same time, Longarm dropped the paddle in the boat and reached for his own long gun.

"Girl, get your head down!" He racked a shell into the Winchester's breech, aimed, and fired at the same time that the rifle of the shooter behind the tree flashed and smoked.

Longarm merely blew up a dogget of gray wood from the bole of the dead tree as the black-hatted shooter drew his head down behind it. As Lacy cowered in the middle of the boat, the lawman fired twice more, blowing up more dead wood. More guns popped around the black-hatted man, smoke puffing from behind aspens, boulders, and fallen logs for a thirty-yard stretch along the northern shore.

"Ah, shit," Longarm raked out, ejecting the spent shell to ping onto the boat floor behind him, "here's your friends, Miss Lacy!" He fired two shots quickly. "Don't you wanna say hi?"

Her only reply was a sob as she cowered, arms over

her head, knees drawn toward her chest, at the bottom of the boat.

Longarm fired two more rounds as bullets sizzled around him, several plunking into the side of the boat with hollow thumps. He doffed his hat and crouched as low as he could, trying to keep his head below the gunwale. Quickly, he thumbed fresh cartridges through the Winchester's loading gate as the guns continued to crackle along the shore.

The boat rocked and jerked as the slugs hammered it. It rumbled over and against rocks but generally stayed on course. A man on the shore yelled beneath the cracks of rifle fire, "Throw that little bitch on out here, Longarm, and we'll leave you on your way!"

Lacy cried out as though she'd been slapped.

"Damn tempting!" Longarm spat through gritted teeth, glancing at her as he snaked the rifle over the gunwale. Taking quick aim, he fired three rounds. He evoked a yelp from behind a lightning-topped cottonwood and blew a hat off a head, but otherwise he doubted he did much damage from this distance and his moving perch.

"Come on, ya crazy star packer!" came another shout from shore. Longarm looked up to see a bespectacled man in a black opera hat and a black shirt with white polka dots on one knee beside a boulder. "Don't die for that little witch. She ain't worth it!"

"I'll say," Longarm raked out again while Lacy just sobbed and drew her limbs tighter to her body.

He fired two more shots, driving the man in the black shirt—Heck Gunn himself—back behind his boulder. As more lead hammered the boat and splashed into the water around it, Longarm returned fire. Soon, however, the boat was fifty yards beyond the shooters and their shots were landing wilder and wilder, as were his own.

Longarm scanned the shore sliding back behind him. Gunn and Cruz's men scurried along the shore, a few slinging lead that dropped well behind the boat while the others were jogging along the rocky shore, sort of dancing around boulders and fir trees, trying to get another clear shot.

They couldn't come far upsteam, however, because there was a large thumb of rock before them—the bulging face of a high ridge. Two of the ambushers climbed the rock a ways and slung a couple of more rounds, but now they were only venting their frustration.

Longarm lowered his smoking repeater and ran his sleeve across his sweaty forehead. He gave a ragged sigh of relief, looking back once more to see the cutthroats gathering along the shore, gesturing wildly, angrily, trying to figure out what their next course of action should be.

"Well, looks like we're out of the woods again," he said, resting his Winchester across his thighs and thumbing fresh cartridges through its loading gate.

"Yeah, but not for long."

Lacy knelt near the front of the boat, staring forward. Her voice had owned a chilling flatness. Looking beyond her, Longarm saw why. About fifty yards before them, the river dropped eerily out of sight.

He dropped the Winchester as he grabbed both sides of the boat and rose to a crouch, staring ahead and hoping that what he was seeing was merely a mirage—a trick of the midmorning light on the water. But, no—the boat was drifting closer and closer to the falls, near enough now that Longarm could see beyond the base of it to where the river continued, stitched with shiny rapids.

His heart fell. His mouth went dry. It was a good fifty-foot drop. The boat wouldn't make it. At least, it wouldn't reach bottom without being turned into toothpicks . . .

Just as Longarm started to scramble to pick up the paddle and try to get the boat turned toward shore, the current grabbed them like a defiant hand and pulled them a little harder toward the drop between two hulking, pale boulders around the base of which water rose like windblown feather nests. It acted like a funnel, and suddenly the boat was caught within the sides of the funnel, and it was being poured along with the main current over the incline.

Lacy looked back at Longarm, her face white as a sheet, chin hanging, silently beseeching him to do something. But about all he could do at the moment was grab both sides of the boat and yell, *"Hold on!"*

As the prow plunged nearly straight down, the girl screamed. Longarm fully expected the boat to crack up in the next second, but after it had dropped about ten feet, shaking him and Lacy like dice in a cup, it got wedged at a slant between two half-submerged boulders.

The river pushed from above and behind, and the boat inched forward with a grating shudder while Longarm dropped to both knees in the middle of the boat and leaned ahead to grab Lacy, who had been thrown half out of the boat upon impact with one of the boulders. When he got her back in, her head was soaked, hair basted to her head, and she gave another scream as the boat lurched forward and then plunged once more.

"Ahhh, shee-ittt!" Longarm shouted as sheer gravity hurled him headfirst out of the boat. As he turned a forward somersault about six feet over the boat that disappeared in a spray of white foam ahead and below him, he caught a glimpse of Lacy disappearing into the foam just behind it. Longarm watched a half-submerge boulder sliding past him as he dropped like a stone into the water on the other side of the rock.

The cold water was like a giant fist clenched around him. Submerged in its icy, churning embrace, he fought to twist around and lift his head as one foot was rammed painfully against a submerged rock. When he finally did get his head above the torrent—at least, it felt like a torrent now that he was in it though the falls hadn't looked nearly as high or as perilous a few moments ago—he found himself being jerked unceremoniously to the right.

A trough of fast-moving, stone-colored water grabbed him violently and hurled him down it. And then another one grabbed him and did the same, though by the time he'd been tossed about by the fourth trough, he realized he was at the bottom of the river and being swept downstream.

At the same time, the current relented somewhat, and he found that he was able to swim a little. Shaking the water from his hair and eyes, he looked around.

Lacy's head and shoulders were twisting and turn-

ing about fifteen feet to his right, and beneath the con-
stant chug of the river, he could hear her screaming
though just barely. Her mouth formed a black circle in
the pale oval of her face and amidst the spitting foam.

"Long-arrrrmmmm!" she screamed louder now.

"Throw your arms out, head back," he shouted,
"and *float!*"

That's what he did, as he knew it was no use trying
to make it over to her. Each of the two separate cur-
rents they were in was too strong. So he let the river
carry him, weaving him between rocks and half over
a boulder. He nudged another painfully with his shoulder, but then he watched the banks widen and the
stream flatten out somewhat, and suddenly, his boots
and then his knees were raking the bottom.

The water continued to push him along but now,
finally, he was able to fight it back, and gain some footing. It was still like a fighter beating against him, but
he stood and stumbled forward, weighed down by his
dripping clothes and brushing the hair from his face
with his hands, looking around.

Lacy was ahead and to his right about thirty yards,
pinned against a boulder out where the water appeared
a little deeper, the current there still strong. She hugged
it like a lover, half facing him, looking at him beseechingly.

"Hang on!" He waded through the hip-deep water,
feeling the river inch up his chest, but it had only
reached his sternum by the time he reached the girl.
He wrapped his arms around her, peeled her own arms
from around the rock, and sort of dragged her back
into shallower water.

For several minutes they knelt in the shallows, gasping. Longarm was shivering. It was a bright, sunny day, but the temperature was probably only in the fifties or so, and the water was probably about forty. He shrugged out of his heavy coat that had threatened to drag him to the bottom of the stream, and as he was about to toss it onto the bank in front of him, he froze.

Lacy must have seen them then, too—two hard-looking, bearded men in battered hats and checked shirts, kneeling along the top of the bank, regarding them both obliquely. The girl stopped shivering long enough to gasp.

Chapter 12

Longarm held on to his coat but automatically slid his right hand toward the pistol on his right hip, then hooked his thumb over the buckle of his cartridge belt. He stared at the two men—a younger man and an older one—watching him and Lacy with cow-stupid expressions on their bearded faces.

"Hidy," Longarm said, walking toward the shore and tossing his coat onto the bank.

"You two shore took a swim," said the older gent, who knelt atop the bank nearest Longarm, absently pulling at weeds with a knobby hand. "Chilly time o' the year for it."

"It was sort of an accident."

"Well, I guess it was!" said the older man, who had one steely-blue eye while the other one was nearly white, and it wandered. He had a thick southern accent, and he worked his gray-bearded jaws on a wad of chew bulging one cheek. A stream of the brown stuff dribbled down one corner of his mouth to add to the stain in his beard that hung nearly to his breastbone.

Longarm saw that the eyes of the younger man were on Lacy. Of course they were, but it made him edgy. He doubted his wet pistol would fire, as water had likely leaked into at least some of the cartridges. He'd lost his rifle along with his saddlebags and bedroll in the river.

"Pa?" a hoarse voice shouted somewhere behind the quartet of bearded starers. "Pa—what's so god-damn fascinatin' over there?"

Longarm saw movement behind the older man, who was likely in his fifties or early sixties—and he watched as a big figure dressed similarly to him and the younger man strode up toward the bank, moving through the hock-high bunchgrass and sage and weaving amongst the pines. Longarm couldn't determine the sex of the person until she stopped just behind the old man, and tipped a broad-brimmed brown felt hat back off her high forehead.

Then Longarm saw the fleshy, pale female features and the two large, doughy lumps behind her gray workshirt, which she wore under a duck coat and suspenders.

"What in tarnation do we have here?" she said, setting her gloved fists on her hips. Her coat and wool work trousers were peppered with sawdust. "Where in God's green earth did you two come from?"

Longarm figured it was probably obvious, but the old man said, "They come down the river, May. Both of 'em. Said they had an accident."

"An accident? Well, I'll say they've had an accident.

Look at these two!" The big woman with mannish features called May wobbled her big, broad hips and long, fat legs down the bank, her large pale face flushing with exertion. "And you two just standing there like lumps on a consarned log! Come here, child—come to May," she said, standing at the edge of the stream and extending her thick arms toward Lacy. "My goodness gracious, you look about frozen *solid*!"

Shivering, blue lips quivering, Lacy gained her feet and, her own heavy coat hanging like wet concrete off her shoulders, walked slowly toward May. "I . . . I sure am cold," she said. "S-sure . . . sure could use a hot fire, Miss May. Maybe a hot cup of coffee . . ."

"Sure, sure," May said. "We'll get you back to the cabin and get you in front of a hot fire. But first, let's get this big, wet coat off of you. Why, it's only makin' you colder, isn't it, child?"

"I'll say it is," Lacy said, thoroughly enjoying the ministrations of the big woman.

The young man and the older man continued to ogle Lacy, as though they'd never seen a female, much less one who looked like her, before in their lives. When May got the coat off of Lacy's shoulders, revealing the wet shirt clinging sinfully to the girl's spectacular breasts, clearly delineating each one, hard nipples pushing against the cloth from behind, Longarm saw their cheeks and ears turn as red as a hot fire.

"Help me here, Felix!" May said as she clumsily led Lacy up the bank.

The rawboned young man scurried over to grab the woman's proffered hand and arm, and, grunting, pulled her and Lacy up the bank. The big woman blew like a winded mule, flushed, and glanced over her shoulder at Longarm. "You'd best come, too, mister . . . whoever you are. Gonna catch your death of cold out here. You'll be welcome in the cabin just yonder. I'll stoke the fire, make you all some hot coffee with a nip of brandy, if you're of a mind for some o' the demon juice!"

She laughed at that, then, draping an arm over Lacy's shoulders, continued leading her off through the pines, the hunched blond looking doll-sized beside her.

Longarm stood where he was, regarding the old man and the younger man before him. They were both big men, he saw now that the older man was also standing. The old man was big and stringy while the young was big and beefy and hard-muscled, though his eyes bespoke about as many brains as could be poured into a sewing thimble. That and the look that Felix had for Lacy's comely figure had the nerves in Longarm's trigger finger sparking. He didn't want this to be another time the girl's female assets put a wrench in his own plans for . . .

The old man beckoned as he, too, watched the girl walk away from the river with the woman he'd called May. "Come on, mister. You heard what May said." He chuckled dryly and turned to Longarm. "When May says jump, we ask how high—don't we, Felix?"

But the boy was still watching Lacy, transfixed, with his lusty cow eyes, and hadn't heard the question. He kept clenching and unclenching his fists aggressively. Longarm took note of that, too, but he was glad to see that he wasn't armed with either gun or knife. The older man, though, sported a Smith & Wesson

Model 2 army pistol wedged behind the wide, brown belt encircling his lumpy waist, the gun's rosewood grips angled toward the belly pushing out his work-shirt.

Longarm picked up his coat and, trembling from the cold water soaking every inch of him, climbed the riverbank, his boots squeaking, water bubbling out from the soles. "Name's Long," he said, sitting down on the bank to wrestle one of his boots off. "Custis Long. Deputy United States marshal out of Denver."

"You don't say?" said the older gent. "A real hon-est-to-gosh federal badge toter?"

"That's right." Longarm emptied the water out of the boot. A good pint must have splattered onto the ground as he said, "And you might be . . . ?"

"Not just might," the older gent said, chuckling dryly as he continued to work the chew around in his mouth, "but I am, yes, sir, Harcourt Greer. These here is my son, Felix. May's my sister. We got us a little cabin yonder. Run a few cattle, do a little gold pannin'. This time o' year we mostly sell wood to the miners up and down the river and cut a good bit for ourselves. Gets right cold and snowy up this high, don't ya know."

"The river's right cold now." Longarm emptied the water out of his second boot, then grimaced as he pulled it back on. The water must have shrunk it a size and a half.

"So what brings you down the river?" Greer asked as he and Longarm started walking in the same direc-tion the women had gone.

Ahead, at the edge of the clearing, May was step-ping into the saddle of a stout mule—probably the only beast stalwart enough to carry her—then reached down to pull Lacy onto the mule's back behind her. Nearby was a big lumber dray half filled with pine logs, a couple of more mules standing in the traces. Another mule stood beside the lumber dray, cropping green fescue and trailing log chains. Apparently, the Greers had been in the process of skidding logs out of the forest and loading them onto the dray when they'd spied Longarm and Lacy roiling down the river like driftwood.

"We were ambushed half a mile or so upriver," Longarm said, feeling every muscle in his body quivering as though he'd been lightning struck. "By the same gang I pulled Lacy out of. To make a long story short, Mr. Greer, we might have brought trouble, so we'd best not linger and make it your trouble. But I would appreciate an opportunity to get dried out and have a cup of coffee in front of a hot fire."

"Ah, hell, don't you worry none, Marshal," Greer said. "Me, May, an' Felix are accustomed to trouble. Why, this part of the Sawatch is rife with outlaws of every stripe—most of 'em cattle rustlers. But there's plenty of claim jumpers in these parts, too, and we're handy at runnin' 'em off. My boy here ain't a cold-steel artist or nothin' like that, but he knows his way around a Winchester."

He glanced back at the beefy younker trailing him and Longarm by about ten feet. "Ain't you, boy?"

Felix grunted. Longarm wasn't sure he could speak. He was staring broodingly after May and Lacy, chewing his lower lip as though he wanted to eat it.

As Longarm and Greer walked past the dray, Greer

glanced over his shoulder again and said, "Get back to work, boy. Excitement's over now, hear?"

Felix stopped dead in the trail, looking as though he'd been slapped.

"But, Pa," he protested, "I wanna go on back to the cabin with you. Why . . . why . . . we ain't had company in a month of Sundays!"

Greer puffed his chest up and clenched his fist at his sides as he fairly roared, "You go on back to work and get your mind off that girl, an' be quick of it! You mind your manners and quit thinkin' about stickin' your pecker in that girl. She's too damn good for you, ya damn cork-headed fool!"

The son of Harcourt Greer cowered like whipped dog, hanging his head like his neck was broken. Cursing and grumbling, he swung around and ambled off to where the single mule stood trailing the log chains.

Greer chuckled as he and Longarm set off again, following a two-track trail through the pines and into what appeared a deep cleft in the nearly solid wall of mountain that stood on this side of the river. "I do believe he's taken a fancy to your girl, there, Marshal."

"Most do," Longarm said, then spat river grit to one side of the trail. He walked with his heavy, sodden coat thrown over his left shoulder, only half paying attention to Greer as he brooded over Heck Gunn and Orlando Cruz and the fact that he now only had his Colt to defend himself and Lacy with. He sure wished he hadn't lost his rifle in the river.

"Well, she sure is a fine-lookin' little thing—I'll give her that." Greer led Longarm under a timber ranch portal and into the cabin yard tucked back in the pines, against the base of the rocky, pine-forested mountain wall. "I tell you, when I seen her take off that coat, I myself thought my old ticker was gonna give out on me!"

Longarm stopped as they passed a corral and small stable and faced the bearded, wandering-eyed man, squinting an eye to more forcefully get his point across. "Greer, I appreciate what you're doin' here, but let me make one thing clear. That girl in there may look like butter wouldn't melt in her mouth. But she's evil. I don't believe in witches. At least, I didn't till I met Lacy. So, what I'm sayin' is this—you and your boy stay away from her, hear? I tell you that for your own good."

Greer studied him curiously, beetling his gray-brown brows and absently scratching the coarse beard carpeting his weathered, brown face. "Sure, sure, Marshal," he said finally. "I understand."

Longarm continued walking toward the cabin, and Greer fell into step beside him. "A witch you say? With a body like . . . I mean, with such an angelic-looking face?" The rancher/woodcutter wagged his head as though genuinely befuddled by the news. "Imagine that!"

The log cabin had a half story and a broad front veranda. Smoke was gushing from the stone chimney that rose along its right end. "Come on in here, now, Marshal," Greer said, mounting the porch steps. "You just go right on in and make yourself at—"

He'd just opened the door but stopped in front of Longarm. The lawman immediately saw what had stopped him.

Lacy stood in front of the fire that was blazing in the hearth, her back to the crackling flames. She wasn't wearing a stitch. Her clothes were draped over a couple of ladder-back chairs. Her full-busted, naked body was pink and perfectly curved. The big woman, May, knelt before her on a braided rope rug, massaging Lacy's belly and crotch with a thick towel, making those perfect orbs jounce deliciously.

Lacy had heard Greer and Longarm on the porch. Longarm knew she had. She held Longarm's gaze for a full two seconds before she gasped in feigned shock but did nothing to cover herself. May had been talking, but now she turned her head sharply to the door and said angrily, "Oh, for goodness sakes, you men! Give us girls another minute, will you?"

Greer stood frozen in the open doorway, one hand on the latch. His shoulders slumped a little, and his knees appeared to bend a bit. Longarm was afraid he'd pass out.

He gave the man's arm a tug. "Come on, Mr. Greer. Like your sis says, we'd best give 'em a minute."

As he led the shocked and confounded older man back out the door, Longarm glanced once more at Lacy. She smiled beatifically. Longarm ground his jaws and latched the door.

Chapter 13

"You gonna be all right there, Mr. Greer?"

"In a minute, I reckon." The woodcutter swallowed hard, blinked at the porch floor.

"You look a little pale."

"I . . . I'll be all right." Greer shuffled to the edge of the veranda and stared off across the sun-dappled yard that was rife with the tang of pine resin. He plucked a handkerchief from a back pocket of his patched trousers and used it to dab his forehead.

Longarm sat in a wicker-bottom chair and kicked one of his wet boots off. "Sorry you had to see that," he said, grunting as he kicked the other shrunken stovepipe off his other foot. "I hope you don't have a weak heart."

"Whew!" Greer chuckled and glanced at Longarm. "That shore was a sight to behold."

"I appreciate your sister's tending the girl. She

really got down to business, didn't she?" Longarm unknotted his string tie and lay it over the veranda rail.

Greer flushed. "May—she's sorta funny that way. Always has been. Never did get married."

"I see, well . . ." Longarm had gotten the drift of May's ways long before he'd opened the cabin door and seen her rubbing that towel across Lacy's delectable body. "Greer, in the interest of my not freezing to death and getting these duds dried out as fast as possible, so Lacy and I can be on our way, I'm gonna go ahead and shuck down to as little as what my trail partner is wearing. I'm just gonna warn you ahead of time."

Scowling at Longarm, who had peeled off both socks and was now standing and unbuttoning his shirt, Greer said, "You know, I reckon I best get on back to my woodcuttin', Marshal Long." He hurried down the steps, boots thudding on the age-silvered boards.

"Might be wise."

"You go on inside soon as you can, Marshal, and get yourself warm," Greer said, backing away across the yard. "I'm sure May'll fix you coffee and a bite to eat. She may be funny in some ways, but she's a right good cook, May is."

"Much obliged, Greer," Longarm said, tossing his shirt over the veranda rail.

Grumbling angrily about Lacy enjoying the hot fire inside the cabin while he was out here turning blue, every muscle and tendon quivering like a diamondback rattlesnake, he peeled his balbriggans down his arms and legs and lay those over the porch rail, as well. He angled the chair in the sun, then sat down in it, stretching his legs out and lacing his hands behind his head, leaning back and absorbing the soothing rays.

He'd just nodded off when he heard the door latch click and the hinges creek and Miss May said in her mannish rasp, "Oh, good Lord—you're naked!"

"Yes, ma'am," Longarm said, glancing behind him to see her standing there, nearly filling the open doorway and blushing. "Thought it best I didn't catch my death of cold." He couldn't help keep the sarcasm out of his voice.

"I've tucked Miss Lacy into my bed upstairs," May said, turning her eyes away from the naked man before her.

"Oh, you have, have you," he said. "Well, don't let her get too comfortable, 'cause she and I'll be hitting the trail soon."

"Oh, don't be silly!" May objected. "After what she's been through? No, sir—she must stay here today and get some rest. I've stoked the fire in my room to try to get the poor dear thawed out."

She turned and walked farther back into the cabin. "I've put coffee and stew on the table, and also a bottle of blackberry brandy. Help yourself. I'm going to see if Miss Lacy needs anything!"

"I bet you are." Longarm heard the woman's heavy footsteps on the stairs that angled up the rear of the room, right of the small kitchen area. Something besides being left out in the cold nagged at him.

Could he be jealous of May?

He grabbed his clothes and went inside. He draped

all the duds over the hearth or chair backs in front of the fire, set his boots on the floor just close enough to dry but not to shrink so tight they wouldn't fit. He sat at the table and the delicious elk stew with crusty brown bread and washed it all down with coffee laced with May's brandy. The rib-sticking meal and warming brandy-laced coffee made him feel less angry at Lacy and annoyed with May for doting on her as though the little witch were royalty.

He piled his dirty dishes in the dry sink, then, yearning for a cigar, he snooped around the place until he found some cheap cigars in an American Powder Mills gunpowder tin. He found a rag and some gun oil in a peach crate serving as a shelf. Sitting naked in front of the fire, where he could easily see the trail fronting the ranch through a window, he carefully took his Colt apart and wiped each piece down thoroughly with the oily rag.

While he worked, and the fire drew the chill river water out of his bones, May came down and, paying Longarm no attention whatever, began heating water on the fire for Lacy's bath. She hummed as she stomped about the place, gathering soap and towels and a plate of food for Lacy, making the floor planks lurch and causing dust to sift from the rafters. Longarm merely chuckled to himself over the bath and continued to smoke and work on his guns and ammunition, keeping a close eye on the trail leading out under the log portal and off toward the river.

When he had the Colt cleaned and loaded, believing that none of the brass cartridge casings had leaked, he slid the gun down in its holster drying over another chair. His balbriggans were dry, so he put them on, and he was glad he had when, after what must have been a couple of hours, he heard voices in the yard. He jerked to life, incredulous at the fading light outside the cabin, and grabbed his pistol.

He slid it back into its holster, however, when he saw that it wasn't Gunn and Cruz come calling, but Greer and his son heading home in the lumber dray trailing the extra mule. May flanked them on the beefy mule. She must have finally allowed Lacy to rest and slipped out of the cabin with the naked man in it, to help Greer and Felix with the wood.

While they headed on past the cabin to the barn to tend the mules and their load of logs, Longarm dressed in his now-dry, soothingly warm clothes. He'd intended to head off today with Lacy in tow, but the swim must have taken more out of him than he'd thought.

He went upstairs to make sure Lacy hadn't slipped out on him without his hearing, as May obviously had. No, she was sound asleep in the big lone bed near a small sheet-iron stove. She lay curled on her side, honey-blond hair sprayed out across the pillow, sound asleep.

She looked like a damn doll. Looks were deceiving. Her clothes hung from a rope strung across the room within about six feet of the fire that had burned down nearly to coals.

Despite himself, he tossed another chunk of split fir on the fire, then headed on outside though not before snagging another cigar from the American Powder

Mills can. He'd leave the Greers a double eagle before
he left here first thing in the morning with a couple of
horses he hoped to borrow. In the mean time, he took
a long walk around, seeing no sign that the Gunn and
Cruz Bunch were anywhere around. That seemed odd.
Had they figured they'd lost their quarry to the chill
waters of the river?

As he strode back to the cabin, he met Harcourt
Greer slouching toward the cabin from the barn. "No
sign of them men after you?" the man said, shoving
his sawdust-covered hat brim back off his forehead,
his wandering right eye angling toward his nose as
though to scrutinize the end of it.

"Not yet."

"Closest place to ford the river is Sapinero, downstream a good twenty miles. We had a bridge but it got
washed out in the spring flood, and, as you saw"—
Greer chuckled—"the river's been high all summer.
Lots o' snow in the high country slow to come down."

"They mighta given up on us," Longarm said, lighting Greer's cigar that he'd only smoked half of earlier,
studying the trail that angled off through the pines
toward the river.

"If they do, you got nothin' to worry about. I got
guns and ammo in the barn, and me and the boy know
how to use 'em."

The woodcutter glanced at his muscular son slouching toward the cabin from the barn, a dreamy look in
his otherwise dull gaze. Felix had probably been
thinking about Lacy all day, as his old man probably
had, as well, after that glimpse he'd gotten of her naked
earlier. Longarm hoped he wasn't going to have to hold

them off all night when he already had Gunn and Cruz to worry about.

"I hope it doesn't come to that." Longarm puffed the cigar again as he turned to the woodcutter. "I'd like to borrow a couple of horses tomorrow morning, Greer. Uncle Sam will pay you for them. Also a good rifle if you have one. I personally will pay you for the grub and the cigars I've pilfered from your gunpowder can."

Greer chuckled. "The smoke and grub is on the house, Marshal. We don't get visitors out here often, and I'm just glad to see someone around besides my boys and ole May, God love 'em. I'll set you up with a coupla fine hosses first thing tomorrow, and I've got a nice Winchester I'll throw into the bargain."

"I'd be obliged."

"Come on in, Marshal. While May throws some supper together, you an' me'll sit out here on the porch and sip some brandy and palaver. What do you say? Like Felix said, we don't get many visitors this far out."

"Fine as frog hair," Longarm said, giving his darkly expectant gaze to the trail to the river once more, hoping he and Lacy were the Greers' only company this day.

Lacy didn't come down for supper. Instead, May brought her a plate of elk steak with all the trimmings and stayed up there a lot longer than was necessary to deliver the plate, Longarm thought. He and Greer and the beefy but bashful boy ate at the table, only Longarm and Greer conversing.

When they were finished with supper, it was good

dark. May hazed Greer and Felix off to the barn, where apparently they slept every night, leaving the entire cabin to May herself. However, she insisted that Longarm sleep in the cabin by the fire to "finish baking that old, cold river out of his bones."

He decided to take the woman up on the invitation. A chill lingered deep inside his marrow. He'd like to stay as close as possible to a hot fire, and he'd like to keep a close eye on Lacy. He wouldn't put it past her to try to slip away from him under cover of darkness.

When May had finished cleaning up the kitchen— she seemed to have boundless, jovial energy for a woman so large—and headed upstairs to bed with her sexy charge, Longarm threw down in the quilts she'd arranged for him in front of the fire. He slept long and hard, basking in the fire's warmth.

A squawk from the stairs woke him. He lifted his head, looked around the dark cabin, saw a big shadow moving toward him. He started to slide his hand toward his Colt when May whispered, "It's just May, Marshal. Fetchin' a coupla logs for the upstairs fire."

Longarm thought with a silent snort, Aren't you and Lacy keeping each other warm enough?

Longarm lay his head back down on his flour-sack pillow. He lifted it again when he felt a draft, as though someone had moved past him. He could smell the must of an animal hide. As he looked up, he saw May standing over him. She wore a big, shapeless buffalo robe.

She gave a grunt and lurched toward him. "Take this, you dirty bugger!"

Longarm didn't see the log she swung at him until he heard the loud clang of a bell, and then everything went dark.

Chapter 14

"Wake up, damn you, lawdog!"

Someone was none-too-gently slapping Longarm's cheeks. The voice and the slaps brought him back to a world of pain and torment in his left temple. At first, he couldn't remember what had put it there, but then he remembered the split pine log arcing toward him. And the pain that followed as he tumbled into a well of hot tar at the bottom of which waited a little man with a hammer.

The little man, grinning, had set to work hammering away at Longarm's head until Longarm was sure that the little fucker had broken through the bone and was whacking his exposed brain.

"I said wake up, damn you, star packer!"

"All right, all right," Longarm heard himself mumble drunkenly, trying to open his eyes.

When he got them open he saw a fist barreling toward him so quickly that he barely had time to take in the broad fingers and bulging knuckles bristling with gray-brown hair, the grimy thumb drawn up tight against the middle one, before it rammed against his chin. He gave a groan as the blow sent him straight back to the floor with another hard blow to his noggin.

It was then he realized he was in a chair. Tied to it with ropes that were cutting into his wrists. On his back like this, he could feel the planks across the back digging into him, the hard, hide-bottom seat digging into his thighs.

He opened his eyes again, grinding his teeth with pain and fury.

Harcourt Greer stared down at him, grinning, showing several gaps in his jaws. His lone eye was still staring as though in bizarre fascination at the end of his nose. The other frosty blue one bored into Longarm.

"If there's anything I hate more than a lawman, I sure don't know what it is." Greer moved chaw around in his mouth.

May's head, her hair pulled back severely from her big, bland, blunt-nosed face. Her eyes were pinched and dark. "Is he dead?"

"Not yet."

Another face appeared in Longarm's field of vision. This one belonged to Lacy. There couldn't have been more of a contrast between hers and Greer's and May's. Her shiny hair hung down, casting her cheeks in shadow. She wore her heavy coat and her hat, as though she were ready to go somewhere.

"Don't kill him," she said. "Let's leave him for Heck Gunn and Cruz. They'll take their time with him, kill him slooooowwww." She formed a red circle with her mouth, then smiled like an angel but with a devil's eyes. "Buyin' us more time to get to those saddlebags before they can."

"I'd sure like to kill him," Greer said, running the back of his hand across his mouth hungrily. "I purely would like to drill a bullet through his head, Missy Lacy!"

"Do as Lacy says," May said. "She knows best. Good head on her, that girl."

"Ah, hell," Greer said, slapping the woman's arm. "Got some other things mighty good on her, eh, May?"

"Shut up, damn you, Harcourt! I done told you how many times to shut your goddamn trap about that?"

"Be quiet, both of you!" Lacy said. "Get finished packing so we can hit the trail as soon as some light shows!"

When Greer and May had disappeared from Longarm's field of vision, Lacy knelt down beside him, gazing at him smugly. "It could have been you, helpin' me go after the money. But, no, you had to be so damn obstinate. Had to be the man of integrity." She lowered her voice to a whisper. "Now, I'm gonna have to cut up the take four ways instead of two."

"I do apologize."

"Tsk, tsk."

"Who are those two, anyways? They ain't really ranchers and woodcutters, are they?"

She smiled again, delighted with her wicked ways. "May said they're from Texas. Bank robbers mostly. They was just hidin' out up here, pretending they were salt-of-the-earth settlers 'cause the Rangers are after 'em."

"We was getting' bored, though," May said as she shoved foodstuffs into a bag on the kitchen table. "We was born bad, Harcourt an' me. Felix was just naturally born bad, too."

The big woman shook her head. "It wasn't hard for dear Lacy to convince me we should throw in with her, go after the loot she hid from Gunn and Cruz." She glanced at Harcourt, who was rummaging around in the drawers of a sideboard near the stairs, tossing ammo boxes on top of it, near a pair of open saddlebags. "If we ever get out of here. Gonna be light soon, Harcourt! Where's that worthless spawn of yours?"

"I told ya, May—he's saddlin' the mounts. Now shut up so I can hear myself think over here!"

"You just lay there and think about it, Longarm. Been nice knowin' you." Lacy touched a finger to her lips, then pressed it to Longarm's. It was wet. Even through the throbbing in his head he could feel the wetness on his own lips and felt a shudder of desire, however slight and eerie.

It angered him. He gritted his teeth and fought against the ropes, but they only burned deeper into his wrists. He rocked from side to side, but his ankles were tied taut to the chair legs, as well, so he wasn't going anywhere.

The struggle kicked up the throbbing in his temple and now in the back of his head, as well, and it nauseated him. So he wouldn't throw up while lying on his back and choke on it, he lay there, sucking air in and out of his lungs and waiting for the pain to lessen.

Lacy went out, and then May slung a couple of croaker sacks over her back and went out behind her.

A few minutes later, Harcourt Greer stood over Longarm, grinning, holding a pair of saddlebags over one shoulder, a Winchester rifle in his hands. On his hips were two pistols—the Smith & Wesson Longarm had seen on him earlier, and a long-barreled Colt in a holster strapped to the man's thigh. "Like I said, I hate nothin' worse than a goddamned lawman. Rangers hung my oldest boy and two of his cousins. Hanged my wife, too."

"I can certainly understand, then," Longarm said wryly.

"I'd put a bullet through your ears if it wasn't for Miss Lacy and the money. Wouldn't wanna do nothin' to get on her bad side." Greer winked. "Until May and Felix an' me get the money, that is."

He cackled, choked, and spat chaw at Longarm, who turned his head so that he merely felt a wetness on his ear as it splattered onto the floor. Then he stomped on out of the cabin, leaving the door hanging wide behind him.

Another wave of rage swept through Longarm, like a wildfire through dry woods. He rocked from side to side, trying to loosen the ropes around his wrists and ankles, but again the hemp only bit deeper into his skin. The exertion made bright roses blossom in his eyes. He ground his teeth against the railroad sparks of fiery pain being rammed through his ears.

He felt like a turtle on its back, unable to right itself. He could only lie here now, hoping the pain died, hoping he could figure a way out of this ridiculous fix she'd gotten him into again. Shortly, he heard horses snorting, hooves clomping, bridle chains jangling. He looked through the open door, saw in the dim, floury light of the predawn three horses and May's mule clomp past the cabin and head off down the trail toward the river.

Longarm growled like a wounded wolf. Like a wounded wolf in a leg trap. He had to get after Lacy and her new accomplices. Bring them down before they found the money and lit out for who knew where.

And he had to get there ahead of Gunn and Cruz. Well ahead. He was outnumbered on both sides, and the last thing he needed was to get caught in a cross fire.

Resting back against the floor, squeezing his eyes shut against the throbbing in his head aggravated by his frustration, he thought, Why not just let them all kill each other? Then, when the smoked cleared, he could take the loot back to Jawbone, and his troubles would be over.

But he couldn't bank on the two factions killing all of each other. One or two could very well make off with the money. And . . . *Christ, could he really be thinking this?* . . . part of him wanted to save Lacy not only from Gunn and Cruz but from herself. He didn't want her to die.

What part of him wanted to save her?

Stupid question.

When he felt the throbbing in his head begin to abate, he looked around and thought hard on how he was going to separate himself from the chair. The ropes wouldn't give. He knew that from the slick, oily blood oozing around them. Fighting them had only cause them to tear into his skin, make him bleed. Since he couldn't get out of the ropes, he had to break the chair apart.

How?

He pondered the question. An answer came to him.

He groaned against it. *This is gonna hurt.*

It did.

Wriggling his shoulders and hips, he managed to roll to the door. He paused there, catching his breath, sweat breaking out all over his body and basting his balbriggans against him like a second, faded-red skin. Then he drew a deep breath and managed to wriggle and roll his way through the open door, then across the stoop and down the porch's five steps.

As he boom-boom-boomed down the steps, he thrust all his weight against the chair until, when he ended up in the yard, he'd busted the back off the chair, and he'd busted the bottom of the chair into two ragged parts. His ankles and wrists were free of the chair and each other, though rope was still tied around each.

Rising, breathing hard through gritted teeth, with that little man busting into his brain in earnest with his angry hammer, he looked around.

It was full dawn though the sun was not yet above the eastern mountains. So far, Longarm appeared to be alone. The ropes were still cutting into his wrists and ankles, but the knots were too tight to untie, so he stumbled barefoot into the cabin, found a rusty paring knife in a peach crate, and sawed through each of the ropes, ignoring the blood oozing out of the cuts in his wrists and ankles.

He had bigger fish to fry.

As quickly as he could in his agonized condition, he dressed and pulled his boots on, wincing at the pain in his ankles as he did. He wrapped his gun belt and holster around his waist, though Greer had taken his pistol. He intended to get it back soon.

Setting his hat gingerly on his head, Longarm looked around the cabin. He doubted Greer and May would have left any weapons lying around. The only knife he'd seen was the little knife he'd cut the ropes with. Deciding he'd have to head after Lacy and her cohorts unarmed, with possibly Gunn and Cruz on his trail, he wobbled out of the cabin, clamping a hand over the goose egg on his temple and hoping Greer had left a horse behind.

As he stepped onto the veranda, frustration bit him once more. The gate of the breaking corral left of the cabin hung open, as did the gate of the paddock off the barn to Longarm's right. Both corrals were empty, and there was no riding stock anywhere in sight.

He cursed and stumbled down the steps and past the remains of his chair, heading toward the barn, and stopped suddenly. Rumbling sounded. He turned to look past the ranch portal. Dust broiled over the trail in the direction of the river. He could see horseback riders jouncing beneath the dust.

Longarm cursed again, looked around wildly, closing his left hand over his holster as though trying to conjure his pistol by will alone. He looked back toward the trail. He could see faces beneath the hat now, which meant they could probably see him, too. Wheeling, he ran back up the porch steps and stopped just inside the cabin door, staring up the trail.

He was almost certain that the hellions thundering toward him were Gunn and Cruz even before he saw Gunn's top hat and spectacles and Cruz's sombrero and short leather jacket beneath crisscrossed cartridge belts. He pulled his head back inside and closed the door. His heart thudded, making the goose egg pulse like a miniature heart, making his eyes water.

He stared out the dusty, grimy window left of the door and watched Gunn and Cruz gallop beneath the portal and into the yard, a small pack of more riders behind them. Their horses were blowing hard. They'd probably been whipping up a furious pace since the first wash of dawn, wanting to get to the place on the river they'd last seen Longarm and Lacy.

The tracks from the river had likely led them here.

Longarm looked around quickly. A poker rested in a box by the cold fireplace. He grabbed it, hefted it. It wasn't much, but it was all he had. If he had to, he'd give at least one of Gunn's crew one hell of a headache.

As the gang drew to a halt in front of the cabin, their dust broiling up around them in the weak morning light, their horses' breath jetting in the cool air, they all looked around the place before Gunn turned his bespectacled countenance toward the cabin and said, "If anyone's in there, get the fuck out here now! My name is Heck Gunn, and I'm here on business. *Blood* business!"

"*Si!*" said his amigo Orlando Cruz, chuckling devilishly beneath his bowler hat and drawing a long-barreled Colt from a holster thonged low on his thigh.

Chapter 15

Longarm stayed back away from the window while edging a look around the corner of it, squeezing the iron poker in his hand, pondering the grim situation.

One thing was for sure—he couldn't allow Gunn and Cruz to trap him in the cabin. He had to get outside and find a good place to hide, though in the back of his shrewd mind he was also trying to come up with a way of securing one of their horses.

How in the hell was he going to accomplish that without getting himself killed? As he stared out the window at the milling gang, a wry grin quirked his mouth corners as the seed of an idea blossomed. Likely a foolish idea that would get him killed, but at least he wouldn't die like a rat in a cage . . .

When Gunn glanced back at the men behind him, and they began dismounting, Longarm ran to the back of the cabin. He opened the back door behind the stairs, stepped outside, and pulled the door closed behind him. He looked around. There was about sixty yards of rocks and scrub pines between the cabin and the mountain wall behind it. About forty yards out from the cabin was a privy.

He ran for it, hearing himself groan as a meat cleaver of pain stabbed through his head. He glanced over each shoulder, spying two of the gang members walking from the front of the cabin toward the barn just north of it, both holding rifles up high across their chest. He fairly salivated at the prospect of getting his hands on one of those long guns.

He came to the privy and dashed behind it, pressing his back to the back wall and turning his head to one side. Two sets of boot thuds rose on the other side, in the direction of the cabin. He could hear someone—it sounded like Gunn—yelling inside the cabin itself, boots pounding the puncheons, spurs rattling raucously.

"Anything?" a man said.

"Nothin' so far," said another. Longarm did not look around the privy but from their voices he knew they were at the back of the cabin, probably between it and the privy.

Silence.

The sun just now rose above the eastern ridge, spreading a warm, buttery light over the forest, thinning the shadows of the pines and firs. Birds began peeping and chortling.

Longarm heard the grind of pebbles under boots, the soft ching of spurs. "Tracks here, Cooter," said one of the men behind the cabin.

The other man didn't say anything. The grinding

of boots on gravel grew louder as both men moved toward the privy. One of them whispered just loudly enough for Longarm to hear: "Stay here—cover me. I'm gonna check it out."

Longarm pressed his back against the privy, squeezing the handle of the poker in his right hand. His heart beat regularly. He could feel it like a needle prodding the lump on his temple courtesy of May. One of the men was moving toward him, then stopped. There was the scrape of the privy door opening quickly, leather hinges creaking. Through the planks behind him, Longarm could hear the cutthroat breathing.

"Nothin' in here," he said, voice echoing hollowly inside the privy. "Gonna check around the back. Stay here so he don't try to slip around on me."

"Got it," said the other man.

Longarm listened to the soft foot thuds. They were coming from the opposite side of the privy from where he was standing. Slowly, he walked toward that side, raising the fireplace poker above his head.

He stopped at the very edge of the privy, holding his breath. As he heard the faint crunch of gravel from just around the corner, he squeezed the poker, tensed both arms. He heard the faint whistling of the approaching man's breath leaving his nose, and then he saw the very front of his black hat brim. When he saw the Indian-beaded band around the hat's crown, and the barrel of the Winchester, he swung the poker down hard.

It crushed the hat and plowed into the skull beneath it with a soft crunching sound.

"Uh," said the man with the crushed skull as

Longarm released the poker, grabbed the Winchester's barrel, and jerked it free of the dying man's hands.

As the dying man's knees buckled and hit the ground with a loud thump, the other man shouted, "Langen!"

Longarm pulled the Winchester back behind the outhouse. The gun was cocked and ready. Hearing the other man's running footsteps, Longarm stepped out from behind the outhouse and over the dead man. Aiming the rifle straight out from his right hip, he fired just as the other man—short and beefy and with a naked girl tattooed on his forehead—ran up to the privy's opposite corner. The man gave a grunt as he stopped suddenly, eyes widening, and brought up his own carbine but not before Longarm blasted out his heart with two well-placed .44 rounds.

The reports screeched around the ranch yard.

The other man triggered his carbine wide as he stumbled backward, dropped the Winchester, and fell hard on his ass, dead before the back of his head hit the ground. Wasting no time, Longarm leaped over the spasming stocky gent and ran around the cabin's left rear corner. He jacked a fresh shell into the carbine's breech as he bolted up the side of the cabin. He ran out into the yard fronting the stoop, to where one bearded man stood holding the horses' reins. The man tensed when he saw the lawman, and he started to raise the carbine he held down low in his right hand.

Longarm fired from the hip once more. The bearded gent dropped the horse's reins and stumbled straight backward, both eyes rolling up in their sockets as though to inspect the quarter-sized hole in the middle of his forehead. Even before he dropped, Longarm lurched forward to grab the reins of a prancing coyote dun.

As he poked his boot through a stirrup, he looked around quickly to see several men running toward him from various points around the yard. Boots thundered inside the cabin, and Longarm jerked a look over his shoulder to see a man with long, curly red hair and a red bowler hat bolting out the cabin door and onto the stoop, wielding two silver-chased Buntline Specials.

"What the *fuck*?" he shouted, eyes finding Longarm and blazing as he raised both poppers.

Longarm set the barrel of his carbine across his left forearm and fired once, twice, three times, blowing the red-haired man back inside the cabin and triggering the Buntlines into the ceiling. The eight horses scattered in all directions, trailing their reins, as Longarm threw down on one cutthroat running at him from his left and ground his heels into the coyote dun's flanks. The dun gave a shrill whinny, buck-kicked, and lunged into a long-legged gallop toward the ranch portal.

Longarm's two rounds blew up dirt to either side of the man running from his left, causing the man to wheel, run back in the direction he'd come from, and dive over a stock trough just as Longarm's third round blew up water inside it. As the lawman crouched low in the saddle and gave the angry dun its head, he shoved the carbine into the dun's saddle boot and glanced over his shoulder. Gunn and Cruz's men were running in circles in front of the cabin, shouting after their fleeing horses.

Gunn himself ran toward Longarm, shouting something that the lawman couldn't hear above the thudding and blowing of the galloping dun, but the man's tone told Longarm that he must have confiscated Gunn's own horse. The man snapped off several rifle rounds, but the bullets blew up dust short and wide. And then Longarm and the dun were hustling around a broad bend in the trail, and the pines closed off his view of the ranch and the enraged outlaws.

"Whew!" he said, glad to be out of there.

But tempering his relief was the continuous ache in his head. The pain spasms were in time with each lunge of the dun, and while he wanted to slow the mount to save them both, he had to put some distance between himself and the gang and then try to cover his trail so they couldn't follow him. He needed to lose them and catch up to Lacy and the Greers, but that would be all the more problematic with the enraged Heck Gunn breathing down his neck.

When he got to the river, he checked the dun and looked around. Obviously, he couldn't return to the San Juan valley, where Lacy had hid the loot, the same way he'd come. But there must have been a horse trail through the rugged peaks along both sides of it, because Gunn and Cruz had managed to follow them and even get ahead of them. Maybe if he rode upstream along the southern bank, he'd run into a trail. He let his voice trail off as he stared down at the ground. His dun picked up an optimistic rhythm when he saw the prints of several shod mounts etched in the forest duff along the river, heading upstream.

He'd just run into Lacy and the Greers' prints.

"Hyahh!"

He whipped the rein ends against the dun's flanks

and tore off along the river. He followed the tracks that
he lost a couple of times due to his speed and when
the trees and brush thickened, but he picked up the
sign once more along a faint game trail. The trace rose
and fell through the rugged country that lifted steadily,
sometimes steeply, back toward where he and Lacy
had put in the river.

Several times he stopped to wave leafy branches
across his and Lacy and the Greers' trail, trying to make
it as hard as possible for Gunn and Cruz to follow.

At the top of a pass sheathed in firs and tamaracks,
he paused to give the tired dun a breather. Quickly, he
gathered dry wood in a nest of rocks and built a small
fire. In the saddlebags and war sack he'd confiscated
along with the fine coyote dun, he found a wealth of
cooking supplies, grub, a bag of Arbuckles, and even
a bottle of whiskey wrapped securely in a scrap of old
quilt. He boiled coffee and drank it liberally fortified
with the busthead, and had a satisfying lunch of the
roasted rabbit—likely leftovers from the cutthroats'
previous night's supper—which he found inside a
peach tin.

When he'd finished his meal, the throbbing in his
head had abated to a slight rapping that he could sup-
press beneath the prospect of running Lacy and her
foolhardy companions to ground. As long as he could
stay ahead of Gunn and Cruz. Staring along his back
trail, he buckled the dun's latigo strap and shoved the
bit into the horse's mouth, the dun swishing its tail and
nickering skittishly at the stranger tending him.

Gunn and Cruz had probably run down their mounts
by now and were hitting the trail hard. He had to

assume they were behind him. They were too seasoned not to have picked up the sign despite Longarm's efforts to cover it.

He swung into the leather, touched the butt of the carbine poking up from the scabbard over the dun's right wither, and put the horse up the trail, casting frequent looks behind him. He kept a sharp eye ahead, as well, for Lacy and the Greers had only about a two-hour head start, and he doubted they were pushing as hard as he was. They likely figured he was dead by now and that Heck and Gunn were dancing over his bullet-torn carcass.

He followed the game path up a steep, grassy mountainside toward scattered pines and a black granite outcropping beyond. A rifle shot flatted out over the top of the ridge he was on. He reined the dun down quickly, shucked the carbine, and cocked it one-handed.

Chapter 16

Longarm sat listening, holding the Winchester barrel up, butt pressed against his right thigh, index finger curled through the trigger guard. Another rifle shot cracked hollowly, the report turning shrill before fading.

Longarm eased the pressure on his trigger finger. The shooter was down in the valley on the other side of the ridge he was climbing. Maybe a hunter. Or maybe one of the Greers . . .

He depressed the carbine's hammer, rested the rifle across his saddlebows, and clucked the dun into motion. It continued following the slanting game trail up across the ridge and into the pines where chickadees and nuthatches peeped in the branches around him, and squirrels, interrupted in their work, scolded him raucously.

He gained the top of the ridge an hour later. The sun was a large, pink balloon in the west, hovering just above the ridgetops. The river that he and Lacy had had their adventure on lay to the north, on Longarm's right. He could see only slate-gray glimpses of it showing between ridges.

A couple of hours ago, the trail had swerved away from it, and now he figured he was somewhere north of the cabin from which he'd plucked Lacy from her dead beau's hard-case companions. To the west lay the gentle swell of a broad valley carpeted in evergreens, the far side rising to bald, stony ridges.

He could see little but the tops of the trees turning dark now as the sun set, but as he stared from a nest of rocks at the top of his own ridge, the coyote dun cropping grass contentedly behind him, he could see a thin tendril of smoke rising from the valley floor. He stared at the smoke. The goose egg on his temple pulsated expectantly.

Lacy and the Greers?

Damn possible. Of course, he wouldn't know for sure until he'd checked it out.

He climbed down out of his nest and walked over to the horse. He ran his hand down the dun's sleek neck, patted its wither. The horse blew softly, becoming more accustomed to the strange rider who'd been forking his saddle for the past eight hours.

"Come on, boy," Longarm said, touching heels to the animal's flanks. "We'll rest soon. Might even have us a warm fire."

His jaws set with purpose, the lawman put the horse down the ridge to the southwest, following the same game path he'd been following the past several hours. Tall trees and the tang of pine and deep, moist forest duff rose around him. He and the dun curved through the ever-darkening forest until they gained the valley floor. Then they followed a fairly straight line through the deep woods. They crossed a shallow creek, climbed a low ridge, and descended the other side.

A half hour later, near good dark, Longarm stopped the dun. The smell of burning pine touched his nostrils. The dun smelled it, too, and was about to give an eager whinny at the prospect of rest and a feedbag and fresh water, but Longarm, long used to the ways of horses, reached around its neck and clamped his hand over the beast's snout, rendering the whinny stillborn on the gelding's leathery lips.

"Patience, partner," he said softly in the dun's twitching right ear.

He swung out of the saddle, tied the horse to a low branch, and shucked his carbine. He levered a shell into the chamber, then off cocked the hammer as a wolf howled somewhere on the far side of the valley over which the night was closing fast. The dun was staring in the wolf's direction with understandable interest, but the horse merely twitched its ears and did not whinny.

"Good boy," Longarm whispered and strode forward, walking softly through the maze of black tree columns. Pine needles crunched beneath his boots, but he otherwise moved soundlessly, something he'd learned in his years of manhunting.

He followed the gradually intensifying smell of the wood smoke for a hundred yards, then crouched behind a ragged-topped tree stump. Ahead, across a shallow ravine through which a freshet trickled nearly soundlessly, the water reflecting the last of the green light drifting weakly down from the sky, a fire glowed. It was about fifty yards away, beyond a juniper snag. Longarm watched it through the inverted V of a tall fir and another that leaned against it as though to hold it up.

On the side of the valley, the wolf howled again. It was answered by another slightly west. Longarm tightened his jaws in hopes the dun didn't whinny and give its rider's presence away.

He couldn't see anyone around the fire, but he could see the vague shapes of several horses off to the left of it, tied to a picket line strung between two trees. Slowly, he rose and just as slowly moved down into the ravine and stepped across the water, trying to keep his feet dry. Wet boots squawked, and mud sticking to the bottoms also made it harder to move quietly.

Ten minutes later he dropped to a knee behind a mossy boulder at the edge of the firelight. Doffing his hat, he peered around the rock. A long, thick lump of a human figure lay on the fire's far side. Probably May. To the fire's left, Greer lay back against his saddle, hat tipped down over his eyes. He held a rifle across his belly in both gloved hands. It rose and fell slowly as he breathed.

There were two more bedrolls amongst the gear strewn around the fire, but they were vacant. Frowning, Longarm looked around. Where were . . . ?

He let the silent question trail off as he heard an indistinguishable sound somewhere off to his right. There was a whisper. He recognized Lacy's furtive voice.

Scowling, he rose from behind the rock and set his hat on his head. He'd wanted to get all four of his double-crossers together, where they'd be easier to corral, but it appeared that Lacy once again was going to do what she could to throw a hammer through his wheel spokes.

He traced a broad circle around the edge of the firelight, set one foot down after another, with painstaking delicacy, keeping to the shunting shadows just beyond it. The sounds he'd been hearing grew louder—sighs of various pitches, hushes whispers, grunts—and when he knelt behind a rotting blowdown slanting to the ground before him, he saw the two lovers moving together, their shadows sometimes merging.

Lacy and Felix. Had to be . . .

Jealousy no longer nibbled at the frayed edges of Longarm's dark soul. Or even at his lust. He'd had his fill of the girl, and he was just glad to see that she was doing to Felix what she'd been doing to him—luring him into her sweet little trap and fucking him seven ways from sundown.

On the other side of the valley, but sounding a little closer now, the wolves continued to howl—sometimes alone, sometimes together. Another one had joined the first two.

Longarm started to rise and move toward them but sank back down to his knee when Lacy said just loudly enough for him to hear: "You like this, Felix?"

"Oh, God, yeah!" the big younker rasped as she rose and fell over him, straddling him. Longarm could see the lightness of her hair in the starlight, very faintly touched by the light of the guttering fire.

Felix lay back against a log, chin up, head tilted back.

"We can do it a lot, if you want."

"Oh, Christ . . . yeah!"

"Shhh!"

"Oh. Sorry."

Lacy giggled softly and continued to bounce up and down on the big, cow-stupid son of Harcourt Greer. Amused, Longarm waited.

"You just think about . . . how much you like this . . ." Lacy said, grunting and sighing, riding the boy faster and harder, hair bouncing on her shoulders. "Tomorrow . . . after we retrieve the loot in the saddle-bags, Felix . . . you just remember what we did here tonight. If we were alone. . . ."

"Huh?"

"You know," Lacy said, "if it was just you and me . . . and the money."

"Oh." Felix grunted, sucked air through his teeth. "Yeah . . ."

Just then Longarm saw a dark figure move in the brush beyond Felix and Lacy. Before he could move, the figure rose up to May's full height, and the big woman said in her hoarse, mannish voice, "Why, you little double-crossing trollop!"

Lacy and Felix screamed as one. Longarm saw starlight flash off a pistol barrel. He bounded to his feet and rushed forward, extending the carbine straight out from his right shoulder, "Hold it, May!"

The big woman was aiming the gun at Lacy's head but now she jerked it toward Longarm, who triggered the carbine, which flashed and thundered. May's pistol popped, the slug flying wide. At the same time, her bulky, dark figure stumbled backward, away from the two cowering frolickers. As May twisted around and dropped to a knee, cursing at the tops of her lungs and clutching her upper right arm, Lacy yelled, "It's Longarm! He followed us! Shoot him, Felix. Hurry!"

The kid must have had a pistol nearby, because his hand jerked to one side and came up filled with steel that the firelight limned like a horseshoe glowing in a blacksmith's forge.

"Don't do it, Felix!" Longarm shouted, honestly not wanting to kill the kid.

"Goddamn lawdog!" Felix bellowed.

Longarm threw himself hard to the right as the kid popped off a shot, then rose up onto his shoulder and triggered the carbine twice quickly.

Boom! Boom!

Lacy screamed as she threw herself away from Felix, whose head slammed sharply back against the log he'd been leaning against. He dug his heels into the ground, lifting his naked midsection and arching his back, wheezing as the blood from both shots pumped out of his chest.

"Pa!" the kid screamed. "He done kilt me, Pa!"

Just then a bellowing roar rose from the direction of the fire, and Longarm turned to see Harcourt Greer standing in his balbriggans and socks, with two pistols in his hands.

The pistols roared, the slugs curling the air around Longarm's head and thudding into tree boles. He threw himself over the now-dead Felix Greer, rolled, and fired three times quickly over the log, sending Greer flying back away from the fire, triggering his last shot at the stars.

Longarm had no sooner fired the last shot than Lacy threw herself against his back and wrapped her arms around his neck, screaming, "I hate you! I hate you!"

She tightened her arms around him, trying to choke him, her naked body writhing against him, breasts pressing against his back between his shoulders. He dropped the carbine, peeled her hands off his throat, and feeling a rage not only for the attack but for the desire she could still ignite in his body after all she'd pulled, he twisted around, swinging an elbow. The elbow slammed against her left temple, and she gave a grunt as she fell against the log with a solid thud. She gave another groan, squeezed her eyes shut, then slumped to the ground, her pale, naked body slackening, breasts sloping to the side.

Breathing hard, still gritting his teeth, Longarm stared down at her. He'd hit her harder than he would have had he not lost his temper. Oh, well—at least he took the hump out of her neck. For now.

He glanced at the dead Felix beside him, then at Greer, who lay on the far side of the fire, unmoving, stockinged feet pointing skyward. Remembering May, he swung his gaze to brush where he'd last seen her, seeing nothing now but brush in the darkness.

He picked up the carbine, rose, stepped over Lacy, racked a fresh round in the rifle's chamber, and tramped slowly into the brush. His eyes swept the ground. Seeing no sign of May, he kept walking through the trees south of the bivouac. The light from the dying fire dwindled though he could hear the soft snapping and occasional popping of the flames.

He stopped, said, "May?" then dropped to a knee and aimed the rifle out in front of him, expecting to see the flash of a pistol.

Nothing.

He waited. Off in the woods before him, a rustling sounded. A low snarl. More rustling.

"No!" May screamed, her shrill voice echoing.

Longarm heard the thuds of several pairs of padded feet, the louder crunching and heavier, frantic thudding of one pair of human feet. A gun thundered twice, flashing on a slight rise maybe fifty or sixty yards away.

The thuds faded. May must have been running down the far side of the rise, the wolves following, trampling brush and snarling.

"Stay away!" May screamed. "Oh, heeelllpppp!"

The scream faded. Then there was nothing but the thrashing and the snarling almost inaudible from Longarm's position.

The lawman straightened, gave a satisfied chuff, then walked back over to where Lacy lay beside the dead Felix, in the same position as before. Longarm leaned the carbine against the log, picked the girl up in his arms, and carried her over to the fire. He lay her down in a bedroll, covered her with a blanket, then tossed a couple of branches on the low, guttering flames. They took to the wood instantly and grew, dancing, causing the orange light to shunt and shudder against the encroaching darkness.

Longarm walked over to where Greer lay on his back, eyes half open, blood oozing from one wound in his right cheek, another in his upper right chest. Two pistols lay just beyond him. One was Longarm's Colt. He picked it up and, looking around cautiously, plucked out the spent cartridge casings and replaced them with fresh from his shell belt.

He rolled the cylinder across his forearm as he continued to stare off in the direction from which he'd come. Were Gunn and Cruz out there? If they were anywhere within four miles of this valley, they'd likely heard the gunfire.

And they'd be riding toward it.

Longarm retrieved his carbine, glanced down again at Lacy, who was still out like a blown lamp. He prodded her lightly with his boot toe, checking to see if she was faking it. He didn't think so, but you never knew with her. He didn't trust her as far as he could hurl her uphill against a stiff wind.

He got rid of all the weapons in and around the camp, including Felix's old Remington, and tossed them into the darkness beyond the firelight, where she'd have a hard time finding them if she went looking. Then he strode off to fetch his horse. He had to get out of here.

He had to take Lacy and get out of here fast.

As he walked out toward where he'd left the coyote dun, he heard the wolves growl and snarl savagely as they fought over supper courtesy of May.

Chapter 17

Longarm led the coyote dun into the camp and dropped the reins. Lacy was still unconscious by the fire. Quickly, he retrieved her skirt, shirt, spare under-clothes, and boots from around where she and Felix had been frolicking, then rolled the clothes up with her in the blankets she slept in. He saddled one of the Greer horses—a claybank mare—before turning the others loose and leading the claybank into the camp.

Gently but not too gently, Longarm picked up the blanketed bundle that was Lacy and slung her over the claybank's saddle. He tied the girl's hands to her ankles beneath the mare's belly. She groaned and shook her head in unconscious protest but did not awaken. He was glad. He was tired of listening to her. He hoped she stayed asleep until they reached the spot where she'd hid the loot from Gunn and Cruz.

He was about to kick dirt on the fire when he tapped his mackinaw over where he usually kept his cigars in the breast pocket of his frock coat and remembered he was out of smokes. This was going to be a tough pull to the hidden loot, and cigars were a necessity. They helped him think. Quickly, he rummaged through Greer's saddlebags, found the gunpowder can and a bottle of brandy, and stuffed Greer's five cigars into his frock coat pocket. He stuffed the brandy into his mackinaw pocket.

Feeling fortified, he kicked dirt on the fire, mounted the coyote dun, and leading the claybank mare by its bridle reins, let the claybank pick its own, slow way through the dark forest, heading toward the other side of the valley. He had to let the horses take their time or risk having one break its leg in the dense darkness that was only weakly illuminated by starlight. As he rode, Lacy riding behind him across the clay's back, he listened for riders along his back trail, though he heard only the wolves once again howling, now with more contentment than before.

It was sort of like him and the brandy and cigars . . .

If Gunn and Cruz were heading toward him, they'd have to take their time, just as he was. Maybe they weren't behind him. If they were, they'd probably wait to track him in the morning.

Or . . . maybe not.

A weird stiffness in the back of his neck told the lawman that the desperadoes had heard the gunfire, maybe even seen Greer's fire, and were heading toward him now. Slowly. Gradually, maybe. But they were back there, only a mile or two behind him. That stiffness in his neck told him so. At first light, they'd increase their pace, which meant he had to increase his, as well.

He just hoped they didn't run him down until he got the loot. After he got the loot, it would be easier to lose them. Now, they knew where he was heading, and it was just a matter of who got there with Lacy first.

He'd ridden for forty-five minutes before Lacy started to groan and sigh, the groans and sighs growing louder until she said in a thick, garbled voice, "Longarm? Longarm . . . what're you doing, damnit. Untie me, damn you!"

Longarm kept riding, putting the dun slowly up the gradual slope of the valley far ridge, climbing through the pines, crossing occasional small clearings.

"Longarm, goddamn your ornery hide, untie me, damn you, or so help me . . . !"

Longarm stopped the dun. With a sigh, he swung down from the saddle and walked back to where Lacy's head hung down the clay's side. "Damn, it was quiet."

She jerked at the ropes. "Untie me, you bastard!"

He would have continued riding with her tied—at the speed he was traveling, it wouldn't kill her—but her screams would give his position away to Gunn and Cruz. He considered gagging her, but while she certainly deserved it, he couldn't bring himself to do it.

Pulling out his folding barlow knife, he cut her free

and pulled her none too gently off the mare's back. She was bound up so tightly in the blankets that she stumbled backward and fell in the grass. "Ouch!"

"Keep it down or I'll bind you *and* gag you, and you wouldn't like that."

"Help me, damnit!" she ordered, trying to wriggle free of the blankets.

He reached down, found an end of the blanket, and gave it a hard tug until she'd rolled pale and naked into the grass, her clothes and shoes tumbling away from her. She groaned and grunted, then cast him a hateful look, jutting her chin. "I hate you, you big, mean son of a bitch!"

"I'm gettin' bigger an' meaner, Miss Lacy. I reckon having done to me what you been doin', capped off by the whack over the head I took from your ole pal May, just made me moreso."

She started to retort, but he stopped her with: "No, no. You just keep that purty mouth shut, or I will bound and gag you. I won't let you go until we get back to where you hid the loot."

Shivering, she wrapped the blankets around her as she sat on her naked rump in the grass. "If you think I'm going to show you where that money is, you're badly mistaken."

"If you don't show me where the money is, Lacy—"

"Yes?" she interrupted insolently. "What are you going to do about it? Spank my bare bottom? You'd just love that, wouldn't you?"

"Nothin' would please me more." Longarm shucked his Colt and spun the cylinder, making it whine. Then he aimed the pistol at the girl's forehead and clicked back the hammer. "Nothin' more except puttin' a bullet between those purty, evil eyes of yours, that is."

She stared at the gun aimed at her from a foot away. "You wouldn't dare!"

"After that last stunt you pulled," he said with a caustic chuckle, "you bet I would. Now, get dressed. We're wastin' time. Gunn and Cruz are likely behind us. You don't want them boys catchin' up to us any more than I do. Probably less than I do, after what you pulled on them." He chuckled again and depressed the Colt's hammer. "Face it, Lacy. You done run out of friends. The party's over. You an' me are gonna fetch those saddlebags and head to Jawbone once and for all."

"Gunn and Cruz are gonna have somethin' to say about that."

"Yep."

She just stared at him, shivering inside the blankets. Her eyes were cold and cunning, just like before. He knew she was still thinking about how she could get away from him. She was trying to put some new tricks up her sleeve. Only problem was, even he himself didn't know if he was lying about drilling a bullet through her head if she didn't produce the loot. That uncertainty was in her eyes, too. Tempering the shrewdness. That was one trick he himself had.

It was about time he had one . . .

"You get dressed and think about it," he said, holstering the six-shooter, then reaching inside the mackinaw and plucking one of Greer's cheroots from the breast pocket of his frock coat. He stuck the cigar in his mouth, then fired a lucifer on his cartridge belt, cupping the flame as he lit the cigar, puffing the aromatic smoke out in the chill air.

She chuffed her disdain for him, then reached around her, gathering her clothes and shoes, then let the blanket slide off her shoulders as she climbed to her feet. Standing before him, letting him get a good look at her jiggling nakedness, she dressed, shivering, glaring at him, muttering oaths under her breath.

Longarm leaned back against her horse and smoked and watched her. At first he tried not to watch, because he feared the warm caress of desire her body evoked in him. But then he realized as he watched her that he felt nothing. No prickling in his belly or cock or elsewhere. He had no urge to grab her and pull her to him, feel those breasts mashed against his chest, or to throw her to the ground, spread her legs with his own, and mount her.

"Here," he said, stiffly tossing her a wool poncho he'd found with the tack he'd rigged her horse with. "Gonna need that."

She grabbed the poncho out of the air and stared at him. She seemed to sense his lack of desire, and it confounded her.

"In rather a hurry to have me cover up, aren't you?" she said.

"Cover or don't cover. Up to you. Just pull that on if you're going to." He stared off along his back trail, puffing the cigar. "We're gonna be movin' again in three jerks of a whore's bell."

With a caustic grunt, wrinkling her nose, she dropped the poncho over her head.

"Sure you wouldn't like one more look at my tits before we got moving?"

"I seen 'em."

Longarm looked at her again and shook his head, amazed that she'd had such a hold on him. Why, she was nothing more than a black-hearted devil standing here before him. All that was missing were the green horns and yellow fangs. She appalled him.

Longarm took another puff from his cigar, then grabbed her and tossed her up onto the claybank's back as though she weighed little more than a small bag of Arbuckles. She gave an indignant squeal at his brusqueness, then leaned forward to grab the saddle horn. "Damn you!"

"Nah, you're the one who's damned." Chuckling ironically, he filed the coal off his smoke with his thumbnail, then, stuffing the half-smoked cheroot in his coat pocket, he took the claybank's reins as well as his own horse's ribbons and stepped into the leather. "You'd best settle in. We ain't gonna be stoppin' much between now and reachin' that loot!"

He pressed heels to the dun's flanks, and the horses moved forward. She grabbed the horn again with a gasp, nearly falling off the clay's back.

The next day, in the midafternoon, he lay atop a volcanic dike in the foothills of the San Juan Mountains, staring through a spyglass he'd found in Heck Gunn's saddlebags. He slid the glass from left to right, scrutinizing a wooded, grassy area along a creek that meandered near the base of the dike. This was where he'd nabbed Lacy away from Gunn and Cruz back in what seemed another lifetime, so much had happened since then.

Twisting the brass-chased telescope slightly this way and that, he adjusted the single sphere of magnified vision, bringing up the scattered pines and piñons running along the creek's other side and up a slight, boulder-strewn rise from the water. No sign of Gunn and Cruz over there. Longarm had thought they might have somehow gotten ahead of him and Lacy and been waiting for them here.

The cottonwoods were shedding their leaves, giving him a good view of where the gang had been camped and the area around where she'd hid the loot with the intention of somehow shedding the gang later that day and returning to it later. Nothing here now but orange and yellow leaves dancing as they fell from the gray-brown branches and flashing in the golden, high-country sunlight. There were scattered piñons, a few wolf willows, sage, and rocks. Not much else to offer cover to possible ambushers.

That Gunn and Cruz did not appear to have set a trap for Longarm did little set him at ease, however. He turned to peruse a broader area around him, beyond the slope on toward the San Juan valley to the northeast, where the Sangre de Cristo jutted against a cobalt sky.

He'd seen no sign of the outlaws since he'd nabbed Lacy from the Greers. His veteran lawman's sense, as well as just plain old common sense, told him they were back there, however. They had to be. That he hadn't seen them only made him all the more nettled, anxious.

Where the hell were they?

He lowered the glasses, looked down the slope behind him, saw the claybank mare and his coyote dun idly cropping the blond needlegrass that grew up from the thin, gravelly soil in front of a low mound of rock. Lacy sat on a rock between him and the horses and slightly to his left, at the base of a small, jagged-topped scarp.

She leaned forward with her elbows on her spread knees, staring at the ground with a wary, crestfallen cast to hear near-blank gaze. She hadn't said more than two or three words to him in over twenty-four hours. She'd been sullenly silent as a scolded schoolgirl, realizing the game was finally over. She looked so raggedy-heeled that Longarm almost felt sorry for her.

Almost.

A hell of a lot of folks had died on account of her, and he'd almost been one of them more than once.

"Get over here," he ordered.

She lifted her head to look at him dully. Then she rose from the rock with a sigh and walked toward him, her honey-blond hair shining in the sun, soiled skirt buffeting about her long legs. Wisps of hair blew against her pale, drawn cheeks. With another, fateful sigh, she dropped to her knees before him, and he held out the spyglass.

"Look over there," he said, canting his head toward the creek. "Point out where you hid the loot, and don't fuck around. Remember my warning."

"Or you'll drill a bullet through my *purty head*?"

"You got it."

She stared back at him, upper lip curled in a sneer. The sneer faded, and apprehension grew in her eyes. She took the spyglass, and aimed it toward the creek, giving it a couple of twists as she stared through it, then handed it back to Longarm. "See that tree with its roots pulling out of the bank?" She canted her head toward the creek.

Longarm nodded. He'd seen the tree through the glass.

"The saddlebags are in the hollow with the roots," she said, rolling onto her side, propped on an elbow, staring off in grim defeat.

Longarm narrowed an eye at her, tapped his open palm with the glass. "They better be."

She scowled at him.

Longarm rose to his knees, grabbed a pair of handcuffs he'd worn hooked over his cartridge belt. "Hold your hands out."

"Why?"

"I'm gonna fetch the saddlebags. Don't want you runnin' off. You're headin' with me and the money back to Jawbone."

She gave him another scowl and looked up at him from beneath her slender, blond brows as he clicked the cuffs closed around her wrists. "It's not too late, Custis," she said with a hopeful half smile. "You don't mind if I still call you Custis, do you? Mexico's a lot warmer than here. Especially, with me . . ."

Longarm chuckled. "You're a stubborn little thing, I'll give you that." He stood, grabbed his rifle, and looked around. Seeing none of the cutthroats moving in on him, he said, "Sit tight. I'll be back."

"I reckon I'll be here," she said with another fateful sigh, looking toward the Sangre de Cristo warily. "As long as ole Heck Gunn don't get me."

Chapter 18

Longarm walked down the steep slope, loosing slide rocks behind him, and crossed the shallow creek. Looking around him warily, expecting guns to start roaring at him from any quarter at any time, he climbed the rise to the pine that had torn its root out of the bank and angled down toward the water. The tree had no bark or needles on it, dead a long time.

He glanced back up the dike behind him. Lacy knelt atop the ridge, staring toward him, cuffed hands before her. Stared toward him with a hopeless air. Longarm turned to look into the ragged cavern where the dead pine's nestled inside the slope. He couldn't see anything, but when he reached into the hollow, pressing his left shoulder against the bank, his gloved hand touched leather. He closed it over the saddlebags and gave a grunt as he dragged them out from behind the weblike roots.

He hauled them out onto the bank before him. The cracked brown leather shone in the sunlight. Both pouches bulged. Longarm unbuckled the flap of one, opened it, saw the green of the paper bundles stuffed inside.

Relief washed through him. He was almost giddy with it. He'd thought for sure the girl would have kept playing games and he'd have to pistol-whip her before he finally found the money bags.

He glanced back at the dike. Lacy knelt as before but she was no longer staring toward him. She was looking behind her, hair blowing in the breeze. Slowly, stiffly, she rose to her feet and turned to stare toward the San Juan valley, then turned her head quickly back to Longarm, snapping her eyes wide.

"It's them!" she yelled. "Oh, God—it's *Gunn*!"

Just then gunfire crackled. Lacy screamed and jerked her head to one side and fell on her side at the top of the dike.

"Ah, shit!"

Longarm threw the bags over his shoulder, picked up his rifle, and ran back across the creek. He climbed the steep slope of the dike hearing the distant whooping and hollering of revelrous riders, the pounding thuds of their horses. When he gained the lip of the dike, he bounded up and over it, and dropped to a crouch beside Lacy writhing on the ground and holding her cuffed hands against her bloody temple.

The riders were pounding toward him up the gentle incline, seventy yards away and closing fast. They were triggering their rifles, and the slugs were hammering the slope around Longarm and the girl, some shrieking off rocks.

"Keep your head down!"

Longarm ran forward and dropped to a knee, firing the Winchester quickly, until the gang of seven riders drew sharply back on their horses' reins and began leaping out of their saddles. Longarm triggered another round, causing one rider to jerk back and yelp. He ran forward to where the dun and the claybank were whinnying and dancing and straining against their reins tied to the branch of a fallen log, in front of the rock mound that sheltered them from Gunn and Cruz's fire.

The cutthroats were shouting wildly, angrily, Gunn yelling, "End of the trail, star packer . . . for both you *and* that little whore!"

Lacy screamed as several bullet plowed into the ground around her, spraying her with torn grass and gravel.

Longarm tossed the saddlebags over the dun's back, then swung into the leather saddle. He shoved his rifle down into the boot, then triggering his pistol to hold the angry horde at bay, he galloped over to where Lacy lay on the ground and swung down, keeping the horse between him and the shooters.

Slugs whined around him. The horse screamed and danced as one bullet tore into a saddle stirrup and another clipped one of the dun's rear hooves.

"Get up there!" Longarm shouted, jerking the girl to her feet, then tossing her up onto the dun's back. He swung up in front of her.

"Hy-ahhhhh!" he shouted, ramming his heels into the dun's flanks and sending the beast flying down over the top of the dike.

The horse hit the slope with another shrill whinny and nearly lost its footing against the momentum of its sudden plummet. Lacy screamed. Bullets sawed the air over Longarm's head. Then he and the girl and the horse were below the ridge crest, the dun barreling hard, grinding its front hooves into the shale and trying with all its might to stay upright as its rear legs scissored, propelling it down toward the creek.

Longarm held the girl between his arms, keeping a light hand on the reins, giving the dun its head. Lacy screamed wildly and flopped forward against the horse's neck, clinging to is mane. As they splashed across the creek and swerved to gallop west along its sandy shore, Longarm glanced behind him.

He couldn't see any of Gunn and Cruz's men, but they continued to trigger lead and shout furiously. He looked forward, swung the dun up the bank, following a game trail that appeared to slant up the slope and into some piñon pines and firs.

"That's my hoss, you son of a bitch!" came a shout from behind Longarm as the dun started up the slope toward the relative sanctuary of the forest.

Longarm looked back to see Gunn and Cruz plunging their horses over the crest of the dike, their riders following in a shaggy line behind them.

"And that's our *dinero*, amigo!" Cruz shouted in his Spanish accent as his sombrero flew off his head to buffet down his back to which it clung by the brigand's chin thong.

"I knew they were near! I just knew it!" Lacy wailed as the dun continued to dig its front hooves into the slope, pushing up with its rear ones. "They're gonna kill us both!"

"Not if I can help it!"

"How can you help it? There's five of 'em, you damn fool!" she said through a sob.

Longarm glanced behind once more. The killers were galloping toward him, Gunn and Cruz out front and triggering their pistols. The girl had a point. He'd faced longer odds before, but Gunn and Cruz and their men were well-seasoned cutthroats.

The deer path climbed to a wagon trail. Longarm swung the dun westward along the trail and whipped its right hip with the rein ends, urging as much speed as he could. The horse lunged ahead, blowing, the air racking in and out of its tired lungs. Longarm gritted his teeth against the sound. The horse had had a tough descent down the slope of the dike and a tough ascent up the opposite hill. Riding double, even with Lacy, who didn't weigh much over a hundred pounds, would be too much for it soon.

"Come on, horse!" Longarm shouted, ramming his heels into the horse's flanks. "Let's *mo-seeeey*!"

Shots grew louder behind him. He glanced back and with a sinking feeling he saw the entire pack of cutthroats galloping along the trail behind him. Their slugs blew up dust on either side of the trail, chewed into trees trunks, snapped branches. They were gaining on Longarm fast.

Ahead, the trail curved. As the dun followed it, Longarm could feel its lunging strides shortening, the mount's knees weakening. He'd decided to stop the horse and make whatever stand he could right here in the trail, when he saw the stone escarpment rising to the right of it. His pulse quickened. He knew without thinking what he was going to do.

As soon as he was around the bend, the gang momentarily out of sight, he gave the reins to Lacy and yelled in her right ear, "Keep going as far as the dun'll take you!"

She'd started to respond when he shucked his Winchester and kicked free of the stirrups, lifted both feet to the horse's back behind the cantle, and threw the rifle onto the scarp. Then he threw himself onto the scarp.

"Longarm!" the girl screamed as she sped on up the trail with the faltering dun, looking wild-eyed over her shoulder.

Longarm grabbed an arrow-shaped point of rock, wrapping both arms around it, hugging it like a lover. His rifle was on the crest of the scarp above it. He gritted his teeth and hoisted himself up and over the rock, rolling onto the top of the scarp, breathing hard, all his sundry aches and pains screaming at him, the pain in his head kicking up again wickedly. Suppressing it, he picked up the Winchester.

Just now, Heck Gunn and Orlando Cruz came into view from around the bend, both men hunkered low in their saddles, Gunn holding a carbine, Cruz wielding two pistols as he cursed in Spanish and batted his heels against his palomino's flanks. The other riders formed a ragged, single-file line behind their enraged leaders.

Longarm dropped into a nest in the rocks about six feet below the crest, raised the carbine to his shoulder, rested the barrel on a stone thumb jutting in front of him, and lined up the Winchester's sights on the jostling figure of Heck Gunn.

He squeezed the trigger.

Gunn's horse—a brown-and-white Indian pony—
screamed above the Winchester's roar as its rider gritted his teeth beneath his top hat and flew straight back
against the pony's rump. As Gunn tumbled over the
pinto's tail, Longarm threw lead at the stunned
Orlando Cruz, who had just turned to his partner as
Longarm's bullet smashed into Cruz's face. Blood
shone like a smashed tomato beneath the Mexican's
right eye, and the desperado screamed shrilly as he,
too, was thrown off his horse's jouncing ass.

Longarm ejected the spent cartridge casing and
lined up his sights on another rider and fired.

Boom! Boom! Boom!

Two more riders were sent screaming back to the
hell they'd ridden out of while their horses continued
lunging on up the trail, one dragging its rider by a boot
hung up in a stirrup.

Boom! Boom! Boom-Boom!

As two more cutthroats were sent to their dusty
deaths, one of the horses pitching wildly, eyes white-
ringed, Longarm swung around to track the last rider
as he galloped up the trail in the direction of Lacy.
Longarm seated a fresh shell, lined up the sights
between the rider's shoulders clad in black leather,
and—ping!

The Winchester's hammer slammed onto an empty
chamber.

"Shit!" Longarm bit out.

Boom!

He jerked his eyes to the rider who'd gotten away
from him. The man's horse had turned sideways in the
trail and was just now lifting its front hooves high off

the ground and clawing at the sky, whinnying shrilly. Its rider tumbled straight back to hit the trail with a thud that Longarm could hear from sixty yards away.

Dust wafted. The horse dropped down to its front hooves and ran off the trail's south side, trailing its reins.

Another thirty yards farther up the trail, Lacy stood in the trail near the splay-legged dun, lowering a pistol she held in her right hand. In her other hand she held the reins of the horse that had only a minute before dragged its rider up the trail. The pistol she held must have been that hombre's, who lay unmoving in the trail to her right.

Scowling in befuddlement, Longarm climbed down out of the rocks and onto the trail. He looked around at the unmoving gang members lying where he'd dropped them, blood pooling in the dust and tough, wiry blond grass beneath them. Gun smoke and dust wafted.

He walked up the trail past the man Lacy had shot out of his saddle and stared at the girl standing between the blowing, sweat-silvered horses. She held the Remington .44 straight down across her bent knee.

"You had the money, two horses, and a pistol," he said, shaking his head, genuinely puzzled. "Why didn't you just keep riding?"

She looked as befuddled by her own behavior as he did. "I don't know," she said tonelessly, hiking a shoulder. "I reckon you could have left me back there, at the mercy of Gunn, and taken the money back to Jawbone." She gave the puzzled lawman a poignant look. "But you didn't." She shook her head. "After all the bad things I'd done . . . you didn't."

Longarm studied her, still not sure what to make of the girl. He stepped forward, wrapped his hands around her waist, and drew her toward him. She stood meekly, almost serenely before him.

"Miss Lacy," he said, sliding her hair back from her neck with the backs of his hands, "you might just make a woman, after all."

"On account of you." She returned the smile, tossed the pistol in the dirt, wrapped her hands around his wrists, and squeezed. "I'd like to be your woman tonight, Longarm." Her direct gaze was serious and genuine, owning a naked sincerity he'd never seen in it before. "Just one more time before you take me back to Jawbone. If that's all right . . ."

Longarm smiled and brushed his thumb against her chin. She looked more beautiful now than she had the first time he'd seen her. "Why the hell not?"

Watch for

LONGARM AND THE DEADLY RESTITUTION

the 410th novel in the exciting LONGARM
series from Jove

Coming in January!

And don't miss

SWEET REVENGE

Longarm Lone Star Omnibus

Available from Jove in January!

GIANT-SIZED ADVENTURE FROM AVENGING ANGEL LONGARM.

BY TABOR EVANS

penguin.com/actionwesterns

GIANT ACTION! GIANT ADVENTURE!

THE GUNSMITH

J.R. ROBERTS

penguin.com/actionwesterns

M455AS0812

DON'T MISS A YEAR OF

Slocum Giant
by
Jake Logan

penguin.com/actionwesterns

M457AS0812

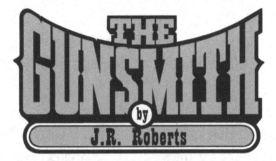
P.O. 0004938097 20200727

M11G0610